ALSO BY

MASSIMO CARLOTTO

The Goodbye Kiss
Death's Dark Abyss
The Fugitive
Poisonville (with Marco Videtta)
Bandit Love
At the End of a Dull Day

GANG OF LOVERS

Massimo Carlotto

GANG OF LOVERS

*Translated from the Italian
by Antony Shugaar*

Europa
editions

Europa Editions
214 West 29th Street
New York, N.Y. 10001
www.europaeditions.com
info@europaeditions.com

Copyright © 2015 by Edizioni E/O
First Publication 2015 by Europa Editions

Translation by Antony Shugaar
Original title: *La banda degli amanti*
Translation copyright © 2015 by Europa Editions

Library of Congress Cataloging in Publication Data is available
ISBN 978-1-60945-268-1

Carlotto, Massimo
Gang of Lovers

Book design by Emanuele Ragnisco
www.mekkanografici.com

Cover illustration by Emanuele Ragnisco

Prepress by Grafica Punto Print – Rome

Printed in the USA

To Giovanni,
for these last twenty years,
and those that will follow.

GANG OF LOVERS

The summer had betrayed all expectations. It had made up its mind to be mischievous, occasionally outright unbearable, forcing the experts to scour the annals in search of another such wet and windy season. That late afternoon the sky was overcast, but it wasn't going to rain. The young man at the table behind me was sure of it, and his girlfriend's nagging doubts were steadily eroding the levees of his patience like a flooding river about to overtop its banks. Another five minutes and he'd be ready to fight. The argument would veer off onto other topics, more serious and personal. It was classic. They were too young, and had no clear understanding of the turns that lovers' quarrels could take. I was familiar enough with that terrain to know that there's nothing you can do but surrender to their inevitability. There's no way to predict or forestall them, they float in the air feeding on trifles, until suddenly they decide to materialize.

Just then, emotionally speaking, I was wandering the desert, and so, as far as those familiar mechanics were concerned, I was an outsider and happy to be one. Still, I felt the need of a lover, any lover, to help fill the void into which I had tumbled.

The waiter brought me an old-fashioned glass filled with seven parts Calvados, three parts Drambuie, plenty of ice, and a slice of green apple to munch afterwards, to help me mourn my empty cocktail glass. We call that an Alligator.

I hadn't ordered it. Danilo Argiolas, owner of Libarium, had sent it to my table. He was a friend and he kept watch over my alcoholic well-being. I had suddenly appeared in his bar in Cagliari, Sardinia, about ten days earlier, after an absence of many years. He'd asked no questions. He'd limited his reaction to reminding his staff that it was no accident that my nom de guerre appeared on the list of house cocktails.

I focused on the ice as it melted in the glass, chilled water pushing aggressively into the alcoholic mixture. For a few seconds it seemed a phenomenon worthy of note, but then that was a time when I was particularly distractable. Out of the corner of my eye I noticed a shadow heading in my direction.

"Are you Marco Buratti? I mean 'the' Marco Buratti?"

"Well, I used to be," I thought.

I lifted the glass to my lips, followed a few moments later by my cigarette, with a languid, studied motion.

"Didn't you hear what I said?" the woman asked in surprise. I hadn't bothered to look in her direction, but it was reasonable to guess that the voice I'd heard belonged to a woman.

"Please go away," I muttered.

Instead, she pulled out a chair and sat down straight across the table from me, so there was no way I could avoid looking at her.

She was in her fifties, and she wore a very good perfume that must have cost a lot, as had the beautician who had worked on her long ash-blonde hair. The dress, the jewelry. And the posture. My instincts as an unlicensed private detective had no trouble informing me that this woman was showing off her money with such nonchalance that she must never have known a time when she wasn't rolling in it.

I had no intention of finding out anything more about her. I wasn't interested in getting to know her. She'd gone out of her way to bring me a case. It was usually a missing person. Maybe her daughter had run away with a stable boy, or her husband had run off with the cook. As I stubbed out my cigarette I mused on the fact that once upon a time, nobody would have dreamed of running away with a cook, male or female. Times had changed.

These days, chefs were stars and they had opinions about everything. Before long, we'd have a chef running the country.

"The lawyer Giannella Marzolo gave me your name," she told me in a low voice. "We've known each other since high school."

In Lugano. Giannella Marzolo had a law practice in the Italian canton of Switzerland. Her office was just a short walk from the Lugano courthouse.

I knew her well: I had been a client of hers when I'd been forced to hide out in Lugano because a group of thugs from the Kosovar mafia were after me. I'd been comfortable there. A nice place—civilized, quiet. I was surprised that I hadn't immediately noticed this woman's Swiss accent, which left no doubt about where she was from.

"It was Giannella who managed to track you down here in Cagliari," the lady went on. "She talked to a guy named Max the Memory. Strange name, don't you think?"

I pretended I hadn't heard her and took another sip of my drink, counting on the fact that before long she'd turn tail and leave.

But that's not the way it went. "The lawyer told me that you'd be able to help me."

"She was wrong."

"I can pay whatever it takes."

"Lucky you."

"I'm begging you, I'm desperate."

"Take a number."

She fell silent, and for the first time she took a good hard look at me. She'd come expecting to find the man who was going to solve her problems, sweep away all her worries, and restore her peace of mind and faith in the future. Instead, the fearless white knight she'd been promised badly needed a shave and had blood-shot eyes framed by deep, dark circles. I lifted my glass in her direction so she could pick up on the slight tremor in my hand.

I was in worse shape than she was. When that became clear,

she lurched to her feet and walked away just far enough to make a phone call. To Giannella Marzolo, no doubt. The wealthy Swiss matron was going to complain that she'd gone all the way to Cagliari to lay out her case before a heap of human wreckage who hadn't even bothered to listen.

A few minutes later she snapped her phone shut and stared at me thoughtfully. She was trying to make up her mind. Her friend the lawyer must have reassured her, based on her memories of a man who no longer existed. I waved her away with my hand. A weary, resigned gesture.

Instead, the lady came back, sat down at my table again, covered her face with both hands, and started to cry. The sobs were shaking her chest. At that hour, Libarium's terrace was bustling; nearly all the tables were taken by people sipping first-rate cocktails and aperitifs and enjoying the view of the city and its harbor. A sudden, embarrassed silence descended. That sobbing woman was decidedly out of place.

Danilo Argiolas appeared beside her and tactfully persuaded her to drink a cold glass of water. "It'll do you good," he added, as he handed her a spotless handkerchief.

My Swiss visitor quickly regained her composure. "Forgive me," she reapeated more than once, doing her best to muster a smile and waving her hands as if she were doing the Charleston.

She waited for the restaurateur to move away before resuming our conversation.

"Something terrible has happened to me," she said, her voice still hoarse with tears. "Giannella insists I should talk to you about it."

"I'm in no condition to . . . "

She raised her forefinger in an imperious gesture. She didn't like being interrupted.

"I kept quiet about a crime and now I've become an accomplice," she explained in a faint voice. "A person may have been murdered, and no one knows about it but me. Out of cowardice

I chose to stay in the shadows but now I have to find out the truth. I can't stand this situation any longer, I'm losing control of my life."

"So go to the police."

"I can't."

I was tempted to ask for an explanation but I managed to quash that impulse. I took refuge in the sequence of gestures required to light a cigarette that I had no desire to smoke. After my third puff I decided to level with her.

"I'm dealing with the aftermath of an emotional collapse, and I'm afraid I'm not doing much of a job of it," I explained. "You just told me that something terrible happened to you. Well something terrible happened to me too. Right now, I'm not even capable of helping myself."

The Swiss woman took it hard. She looked like a promising but slightly over-confident middleweight who'd just taken a right hook to the chin and wound up flat on the canvas. She sank back in her chair, and her eyes again filled with tears.

"Quit your crying," I told her in a fairly brusque tone of voice. "I come here every day to drink in blessed peace and the last thing I want is to make a scene. Word will get around that I'm a guy who makes women cry, and you'd ruin my reputation."

She gulped back her tears. She signaled to the waiter and ordered a Negroni along with a cold, lime-and-basil smoked salmon appetizer. Noblesse oblige. She took a cigarette from my pack and leaned over the table so I could light it for her.

"All right," she said after a while. "You are unable to accept the job I'd hoped to hire you for, but from what Counserlor Marzolo told me, you are a man with extensive experience, a man who knows a lot about the criminal underworld."

"Well, then?"

"You could always give me some advice. Maybe you know someone . . ."

I shook my head. "I don't want to get involved."

Her tone suddenly turned resolute. "I haven't come all this way to go home empty-handed. You're going to listen to me and I'll pay you lavishly for your trouble."

The lady wasn't used to hearing no. Especially not from people like yours truly; according to her, the more you paid people like yours truly, the more we were supposed to hurry up and make ourselves useful. I distracted myself by trying to remember the last time someone had wanted to pay me "lavishly" for my services and my gaze happened to come to rest on a young woman's tattooed arm. A braided vine of red and green flowers covered her skin from wrist to shoulder. Summer made evident the demographic explosion among the ranks of the tattooed. I had nothing against tattoos and, had I never been a guest in Italy's prisons, I too might have been displaying a piece of fine art on my own flesh. But as it was, I couldn't help but associate tattoos with my prison time, and it had irrevocably killed their charm.

"Would you please just give me an answer?" the lady asked in a lightly exasperated tone.

"Tomorrow," I said to get her off my back. "Here, at the same time."

She smiled, shook my hand, and left. Her walk was very elegant, but it tended to restrict the movement of her derriere. I decided that the blame should be placed squarely on the nuns at the boarding school where the poor little rich girl had certainly studied.

I wasn't planning to come back the next day. She'd stand there, looking around, muttering insults under her breath. Lying to her had been the only way to defend myself from her bossy arrogance. If I hadn't tricked her, she'd have forced me to listen to her story, and I didn't have the strength to shoulder the burden of anyone else's personal tragedies.

I'd come to Cagliari to hide out and find some meaning in my life. My new life. Because the life I'd led until just a few weeks ago had been swept away by the waves on a beach near Beirut.

CHAPTER ONE

Chef-Boutonne, France. February 2012.
Sixth year of the gang war.

W e'd chosen the meeting place. Winter nights in the countryside of northwestern France were cold, dark, and lonely. The cops tended to stay inside where it was warm, just like everyone else. There really was absolutely no reason to venture outside. But we weren't bound to the rhythms of the soil, which in that part of the country was covered in fields and vineyards. We were outsiders caught up in an underworld gang war. The kind of brutal conflict that breaks out one day, and no one knows when it's going to end. The kind that takes blood and years of your life, and flushes them down the toilet. Except for the people fighting, no one else gets involved; this kind of battle doesn't make the news. The police don't care, and the press doesn't care. Sure, every so often they stumble across a corpse and someone opens a file and someone writes a headline, but nobody's making it a priority.

We knew perfectly well that there weren't going to be many other gang wars like this one. It belonged to a criminal world that was disappearing, a milieu in which we had operated under various guises for the better part of twenty years. Now that world was falling apart, forced out of existence by organizations and individuals that disgusted us. We wanted nothing to do with them.

The modern world, in that sector, was by then all mafia: multinational, a cross section of every and all kinds of corrupt institutional power. Corrupt and toxic. When enriching yourself illegally means poisoning people and the places they live, devising latter-day slave trades, and working hand in glove with politicians, businessmen, and moguls of high finance, then free men with a conscience decide it's time to leave the party.

The days when membership in the ranks of self-respecting criminals required only that you have nothing to do with drugs or prostitution existed only in the memories of a very few.

At my side, that night, I had one of the last men of that generation: Beniamino Rossini. A smuggler and an armed robber. A man who stood tall his whole life. Nothing to do with the little pieces of shit who infested the environment these days, cruel to those weaker than them and ready to sell out at the first opportunity. Especially to the police.

I hadn't entered that world of my own accord. I wound up in prison more or less by accident, where I'd earned a reputation as something of a peacemaker, and when I got out, lawyers started turning to me to help them solve certain of their clients' problems. Sometimes that's exactly what really happened, but more often matters turned out to be more complex. That old bandit helped me survive. He knew how to be violent, deadly. Characteristics I'd never possessed, all on account of the blues that long, long ago, I used to sing in clubs here and there.

Max the Memory wasn't a man of action either. Now he was smoking a cigarette, staring into the dark. A fat man with pale blue eyes, but with a heart and a brain as vast as the mountains. He'd become my partner after his dreams had betrayed him and he'd wound up as one of those guys who is expected to pay for everyone else.

None of us had ever have expected to be caught up in that war that we'd unintentionally unleashed. All we could do now was fight. Deserting wasn't an option. Nor was surrender. We'd taken body blows and we'd dealt them out, we'd laid low, we'd unleashed attacks. Six long years had gone by, six years of absolute madness. We were exhausted, and all we wanted now was to go back to our own complicated lives.

So when we saw the headlights of a car turning into the piazza, we heaved a sigh of relief. Max and I came out into the open, stepping into the cone of light underneath a streetlamp, while old man Rossini stayed hidden under the portico of the old market, both hands plunged into the pockets of his overcoat, wrapped around the grips of his pistols.

The woman behind the wheel turned off the engine and stepped out of the luxury sedan she'd driven halfway across France. Her name was Bojana Garašanin and she was a dangerous criminal. A made woman, who'd grown up with the cult of nationalist violence that characterized Serbian gangsterism. Short black hair, stout, muscular, rough features. Her mouth was the exception: truly fine, sensual. A touch of totally pointless craftsmanship.

"Where is he?" she asked, pulling the hood of her down coat over her head. Her breath came out in a plume of white vapor.

I gestured at the darkness behind me. "In a car trunk," I lied.

She nodded her head as her gaze wandered. She was probably trying to figure out where Rossini was hiding.

"Let my uncle go. I'll tell you where you can find Natalija Dinić."

One of that woman's many identities. When we first met her she was calling herself Greta Gardner. "Is that the name she's using these days?" Max asked.

"That's another piece of information you'll get when you release him."

"It's not that simple," the fat man explained.

"What is that supposed to mean?"

"Finding your boss, Dinić, isn't really a priority for us right now. First, we want to shut down all her businesses."

She clenched both fists in a gesture of irritation. "That was Sylvie's decision, wasn't it?"

I had no reason to deny it. "She thinks that's the best way to handle things."

Her voice rose an octave. "That means this thing will never end."

"Sylvie is the aggrieved party," I reminded her. "It's up to her to decide how and when to put an end to this feud."

"Natalija too thinks she's been the victim of wrongs that must be washed away with blood. You killed the two men she loved. You even killed the second one at the altar, seconds after he had placed a wedding ring on her finger."

His name had been Vule Lez, and he was another Serbian gangster. As he died, he bled all over Natalija Dinić's wedding dress, in the Serbian Orthodox church of St. Sava, in Paris, before pews full of guests. An execution-style murder that had been strategically important in terms of the feud's outcome. Dinić's first husband, on the other hand, had asked for it. I couldn't even remember his real name anymore, only the name the Serbian intelligence agency had given him when he showed up in Padua. Pierre Allain. This guy wanted to force us to investigate the theft of a colossal quantity of drugs from the vaults of the Institute of Legal Medicine. We'd politely turned down the job, but he had insisted, had made life hard for us, forcing Rossini to shoot him. We'd buried his corpse under the one of the countless new highways being built across the northeastern Italian countryside and had considered the chapter closed until his widow decided to take revenge. In the worst way possible.

"Your boss should have taken it out on us," I replied, "not on Rossini's woman. She had Sylvie kidnapped, she tortured her, and then she sold her to a gang of Kosovar mafiosi. She suffered too much, and now she can't forget."

The woman touched her temple with a brusque gesture. "The truth is that she's out of her mind. Both of them have gone crazy. Natalija lives only to look as much like Sylvie as possible.

She's had surgery three times now, and she keeps staring at pictures of her, trying to figure out new details to copy. Her plan is to eliminate Rossini's woman, but only once she's become her identical twin. And then she'll take care of the rest of you. And what she has in mind must have been suggested by the Devil himself."

I shook my head, horrified. "That's not going to happen. We're going to stop her first."

Bojana smiled. Or rather, she bared her teeth. Tiny, sharp teeth. "Only if I help you," she pointed out. "And in any case Natalija's businesses cannot be part of any deal. My family has decided to purchase them."

"That's a white slave trade racket," I reminded her. "We've already decided to put an end once and for all to the sexual-slavery ring you people have been running for years."

She spread her arms wide. "You're asking too much. My father and his brothers have decided to offer you my boss's life in exchange for my uncle's. But that's it. I know them: if you insist on these ridiculous conditions they'll sacrifice the hostage, even if he is a beloved member of the family, and they'll establish an alliance with Natalija Dinić in order to destroy you."

Max and I exchanged a glance. We were in no condition to fight a war on two fronts and our strategy was crumbling before our eyes. We hadn't taken into account the Garašanin family's greed.

Bojana suddenly stiffened. I turned around and saw Beniamino coming toward us. He'd gotten tired of listening to the conversation through my cell phone.

"Fine. We'll settle for the hide of Natalija Dinić," he told the woman, extending his hand.

She shook it vigorously. "That's best for everyone. I tell you where to find her and you let my uncle go. He must be freezing, shut up in a car trunk."

"The last thing in the world we'd want you to think is that

we don't trust you," I said with a hint of irony. "Still, I think we'll let your uncle go only after all this is over."

Bojana Garašanin shrugged her shoulders. "Well, it was worth a try. And in any case, we'd have certainly kept our word."

"Like hell you would!" snickered old man Rossini. "Now, where is Natalija?"

"In Lyon," the Serbian woman replied, pulling a couple of folded sheets of paper out of her pocket. "I've written all the information you'll need right here."

"You've been her bodyguard for years and years now," Beniamino pointed out.

"Twelve years, to be exact. At first, it was just me, and then Ana came to work for her too."

"That's exactly who I wanted to talk about. Should we consider her an enemy or is she up-to-date on our understanding?"

The woman took a step forward and poked him in the chest with an extended forefinger. "When it happens we'll do nothing to interfere, but remember this: nothing happens to Ana, or I'll cut your throat with my own hands."

Rossini nodded. "I was just making sure. In cases like this, you always risk making mistakes that could make other people very unhappy."

Bojana relaxed. "Follow the instructions and we won't have any problems," she added as she headed back to her car.

I stared at Rossini. "You just shook hands with her."

"That's right."

"That means we're willing to let the Garašanin gang take over our enemy's businesses."

The old bandit shrugged. "We can't save the world, Marco. All we can do is try to put a dignified end to this matter."

"What about Sylvie?"

"Once Natalija is dead, maybe she'll start living again. Though I have my doubts, and the shrinks don't seem especially optimistic."

Max pulled out his cigarettes and we smoked in a silence charged with bitterness.

"If what Bojana says is true, it'll feel like shooting my own woman," Rossini commented.

"Are you ready for this?" I asked. "Otherwise we can ask Luc and Christine. I'm sure they'd be happy to oblige."

I was referring to Luc Autran and Christine Duriez. A married couple, armed robbers from Marseille, who had joined our little army out of a longtime friendship with Rossini. Every so often they'd rob a bank or a jewelry store to help finance our expensive survival.

Beniamino was smoking with his eyes half-shut and his neck tucked deep in the lapels of his long camel-hair overcoat. He crushed out the butt with the heel of his shoe. "It's up to me to do justice."

Twenty minutes later we drove through the front gate of a farm that a real estate agent couldn't manage to sell but had been willing to rent to us for far more than the market price, no questions asked. In the large kitchen, embers still glowed in the fireplace, and the temperature was quite cozy. Max assembled a snack from bread, salami, and cheese.

"Lyon is the capital of fine French cuisine," he said as he fooled around with a corkscrew. "I know a couple of *bouchon*s in rue de Brest that are worth a visit."

"I don't think we'll be there long enough," Beniamino retorted. "And more importantly, it's not like the three of us can be seen at a restaurant together."

The fat man was unfazed. "That just means I'll go alone. And then I'll tell you all about the flavors and smells."

"Stop spouting bullshit and give us the information that Bojana handed over."

He pointed to the down jacket hanging from the coatrack. "It's in the right-hand pocket. And stop insulting my perfectly legitimate desire to expand my culinary and enological horizons," he objected, gesturing with the salami. "If it weren't for me, there wouldn't be even the slightest trace of poetry in your diet."

"Among your many fine qualities," Rossini broke in, poker-faced, "the one I value most highly is your incredibly thick skin."

I ran my eyes over the sheets of paper before interrupting my friends' banter by reading aloud. It was a list of dates and times, all of Natalija Dinić 's appointments over the next two weeks, laid out in a faintly childish handwriting. Gym, dentist, hairdresser, beautician.

Max picked up his iPad and started looking up the addresses on the map of Lyon. "They're all downtown. Narrow streets, lots of traffic, police everywhere."

"As long as it's inside, any building will do. The main thing is to pick the right building for what we want to do," Rossini said as he stood up. He cocked his pistol. "I'm going downstairs to get the 'uncle.' He still needs to eat and he must be curious about how our meeting went with his little niece."

A few minutes later, our prisoner was seated at our table, sipping a glass of red wine. His name was Lazar Garašanin, he was close to sixty years old, and he'd distinguished himself in the civil war that had dismembered Yugoslavia by eliminating a respectable number of Croatian civilians. He considered himself a soldier, an officer, and he put on the airs and demeanor of one. But in reality he was nothing but a butcher.

He and two other "veterans" had kidnapped Sylvie and handed her over to Dinić. For money. Then he'd been hired again to eliminate us in Paris, but he'd made the unforgivable error of underestimating old man Rossini's experience and instincts. He'd watched his accomplices die, and then he'd surrendered. Beniamino had held the muzzle of his pistol jammed against his forehead for several long minutes.

"Unfortunately we need you alive," he'd finally whispered

in disappointment as he lowered the pistol. Lazar had fallen to his knees, sobbing like a baby.

That same evening we'd sent a message to his niece and the negotiations had gotten underway.

"We met with Bojana," I informed him.

"In that case, I'll be going home soon," he snickered nervously, stroking the gray stubble on his chin.

"That depends on how things turn out," Rossini retorted menacingly. "In this kind of situation, it's never a good idea to count your chickens before they hatch."

The uncle turned pale and concentrated on the butter he was spreading on his baguette. "If you had just let my niece take care of things, we'd be done by now," he grumbled unhappily. "A few drops of poison, a silk noose around her neck. Quick and clean."

"We don't hire hit men," Beniamino interrupted.

"That's an offensive term in any language," the offended Serbian protested, shoring up his own self-respect.

"We're leaving tomorrow," I announced, changing the subject. "We're going to leave you locked up in the cellar, with plenty of food and water, and when the time comes we'll tell Bojana to come set you free."

"But that way I don't have any guarantee that you'll keep your side of the bargain."

"Don't tell me you're afraid, 'commandant'?" I asked with a smile.

The Serbian pointed at Rossini furtively. "Yes, I am—of him."

Lazar really was a poor idiot. He was afraid of Beniamino's vengeance because his criminal culture couldn't conceive of the notion of respect. Respect for one's word, for prisoners, for women and children.

The old bandit took him by the arm. "It's time for you to go beddy-bye, Lazar Garašanin. You're no longer welcome here."

The trip to Lyon took more than five hours. In a brasserie on the outskirts of town we met Luc and Christine. They both looked different than the last time I'd seen them. Evidently they'd made a withdrawal since then, and changing your look was essential in the world of armed robbery.

Luc had shaved his mustache, and Christine had dyed her hair a faded red. Both of them wore coveralls that bore the logo of a janitorial company.

"We found a safe house in Vienne," Luc informed us. "The lady that rented to us is the widow of a straight-up guy I met in prison."

"It's more than thirty kilometers outside of town," his wife added. "But these days the city isn't safe. The cops are hunting for a couple of fugitives and they're checking everybody and everything."

Rossini shrugged. "We'll be fast and discreet. Like always."

Max and I boarded a bus and headed for the center of town, where we planned to scope out the places Natalija Dinić was a regular. It was nice to stroll through the streets of that beautiful city, both ancient and prosperous, but our minds were on other things. On the one hand, we were relieved at the thought that this whole thing might soon be over once and for all. On the other, we were filled with a kind of dread completely divorced from rational thought. Even though we knew it was the right thing to do and that there were no feasible alternatives, planning a murder that required a betrayal to work just didn't fit with the lives we'd led up till then.

"That whore ruined our lives and yet an inexplicable sense of remorse will color our experience of her death," said the fat man, between slurps of beer.

"It's a burden we're going to have to share with Beniamino. He's the one who's going to be pulling the trigger."

We had slipped into a bar on rue de la Martinière, where Natalija's dentist had his office, almost right across the street from the Académie de Billard. You had to walk through a small front garden to get into the building. Though we hadn't yet checked the other addresses, we both knew that this was where it was going to happen. It was a sort of no-man's land surrounded by hedges, with a couple of trees that seemed to have been planted with an ambush in mind.

As always, the real problem would be our escape route, but we could leave that detail to the old bandit and the couple from Marseille.

We boarded a taxi and headed to the station. The train was packed with exhausted commuters; some talked on their cell phones, while the rest listened resignedly to bits and pieces of other people's lives.

"I feel like having a smoke and a drink," I confided to Max. "And to think I only quit half an hour ago."

"I hear you. And I'm hungry, too. We just need to fill in the holes in our lives."

I snickered. "You've dated too many shrinks. They've left their mark on you."

"Only the Lacanians. Two Lacanian psychoanalysts, to tell the truth, are plenty."

"If you ask me, you'll fall for a third the first chance you get."

"You can bet on it. Before long I'll climb a tree and start shouting: *I want a woman!* Like the crazy uncle in Fellini's *Amarcord*."

"Life during gang wars." I'd meant it as a cynical wisecrack but it came out sounding gloomier than I'd intended.

"I think you ought to give the idea of a girlfriend who's a shrink some thought," the fat man observed. "If you go on like this, every woman you meet will give you the heave-ho the way that cute bartender in La Trinité did."

"You're a pal." In the past few weeks I'd been doing my best to forget about the latest pathetic attempt I'd made at picking up a woman I liked. It was the end of July, a rainy day that was anything but warm. I'd stopped to fill up my tank and the sign across the street had caught my eye: Tip Top Bar.

I decided that a quick shot of something wouldn't hurt and the next thing I knew I was standing in a bar that was practically deserted except for a couple of retirees, regular customers, each nursing a pastis he meant to make last until evening, and a female bartender who was giving me a level look: arms crossed and a cigarette dangling from her lip.

Forty years old, a cascade of dark curls, a pretty face, made up as if she was waiting her turn to walk the runway for an exclusive Parisian designer. Tits and neckline that you couldn't miss.

"With someone like you behind the bar, this place ought to be packed with horny men," I said after ordering a beer and an anisette.

"They show up after sunset," she replied. "That's when I'm at my best."

"Then maybe I'll wait around for the show to start."

I took the little shot glass of liqueur and dropped it into the mug of beer. By the time it hit bottom, the anisette was nicely mixed in with the beer. "Just perfect as a thirst-quencher," I explained.

She paid no attention to me. She'd already filed me away as just another customer. I started staring at her insistently. She got annoyed almost immediately.

"Something wrong?" she huffed.

"I want to strike up a conversation but I can't figure out the best gambit to attract your attention. I don't want to get my first move wrong."

"Oh, you're a slick one with the girls, aren't you," she said in a mocking tone of voice, before walking over to the radio to change the station.

I took advantage of the opportunity to get up on my tiptoes so I could catch a good look at her butt and her legs. I caught her wry glance as she watched me in the mirror behind the bar. "Everything meet with your approval?" she asked.

"Yes," I sighed.

She tuned the radio to a station that was playing *Coeur de Chewing Gum*. Brigitte sang:

Si j'avais le coeur dur comme de la pierre
j'embrassarais tous le garçons de la terre
mais moi j'ai le coeur comme du chewing gum
tu me goûtes e je te colle . . .

"Is your heart all gummy too?" I asked her.

The woman gestured for me to pay attention to the lyrics.

Irrésistiblement amoureuse c'est emmerdant
Irrésistiblement emmerdeuse c'est amusant.

"So now do you get it?" she asked.

"Yep, you're having some fun at my expense."

"That's exactly right."

"And I deserve it, don't I?"

"Your question about my heart was strictly for beginners."

Just then I felt my cell phone buzz in my shirt pocket. It was Beniamino. He was calling to find out whether I'd crossed the border and when he should expect me in Nice. Staring the bartender right in the eye, I told him that I wasn't far away, but that I would most likely get there a couple of days late because I'd just met the most beautiful woman on earth. My friend asked no questions, it was enough for him to know that I was well and on my way. She, on the other hand, burst out laughing.

"You understand Italian," I said, stunned.

"Enough. Like everyone here, we're just a stone's throw from the border."

"And I made you laugh."

"Am I really the most beautiful woman on earth?"

"Absolutely no doubt about it."

She stuck out her hand. "The name's Ninon."

That was her first name: her surname was Colin. I learned that when I rang her doorbell the following day. The night at the Tip Top Bar had been challenging, both in terms of consuming alcohol and in terms of controlling my anger. A ridiculous number of contenders for her attention whom I'd gladly have gotten rid of by waving a sawn-off shotgun. The lovely bartender had invited me over for lunch, but there was nothing on the kitchen table but a paper sack with two ham sandwiches.

"Wine or beer?" she asked.

"Beer," I answered, absentmindedly. All my attention had been drawn to a poster that showed Ninon, practically naked, feverishly clutching at some man.

"I worked in porn until two years ago," she explained. "And that big handsome hunk is my ex-husband. He's no longer acting either, now he's a producer in Slovakia."

"Will you give me a complete set of all your movies?" I asked, perfectly serious.

"No," she replied, and then she kissed me.

Ninon was beautiful. I'd have stayed in her bed for the rest of my life but there was no room for me in her life. I was just a foreigner passing through, a good way to break up the monotony of a town where all the men were after her but none really wanted her. She accepted the situation because the Tip Top Bar had been in her family for as long as anyone could remember and she wouldn't have abandoned it for any reason on earth.

Two days later I was completely head over heels in love with her. When it dawned on me that my time was up, I walked into the bar and asked her to run away with me. Right then and there.

Ninon lit two cigarettes and stuck one between my lips. "Please, don't be ridiculous. Don't leave me with such a depressing memory of you."

But I just kept making things worse. Luckily she got sick of it quickly and kept me from sinking all the way to rock bottom.

"Beat it, handsome!" she hissed, cold as ice. I turned on my heel and headed straight for the door.

As I walked past the table with the two retirees, I heard one comment to the other: "Another day, another asshole, eh, Louis?"

He was right, and everything about what had happened kept on making me feel shitty. Ninon didn't deserve to be treated like that. This was collateral damage in the war that would only come to an end, perhaps, with an inevitable execution.

At the Vienne train station, we found Luc waiting for us with a small delivery van. The safe house was just another farmhouse way the hell out in the countryside. It hadn't been lived in for years, and there was dust everywhere. Plus it was freezing. The heaters were going full blast, but the place wasn't even going to begin to warm up until the next day.

Max went to help Christine get the kitchen into working shape. I went in search of Beniamino to bring him up-to-date on our scouting trip in Lyon.

The first thing I told him about was the little front garden. He asked me about a couple of details, but only to be polite; it was clear he had other things on his mind.

"You've talked to Sylvie," I guessed.

"Right. I told her that we've been forced to give up on the idea of hitting Natalija Dinić 's business interests and she didn't take that well at all. She insulted me. Every day that passes, she seems to have a crueler tongue."

I pulled a small flask of Calvados out of my jacket pocket. I'd been carrying it around with me for the past two days and I had yet to taste a drop. I unscrewed the cap and handed it to my friend.

He took a substantial gulp. "At this point, everything about this thing hurts. It's just sick."

I agreed, and I sat there listening to his sad, weary thoughts. He despaired over the woman he loved, who could no longer find anything to care about in her life.

"The only thing about me that she loves is the violence I can unleash on her enemies."

"They're your enemies too. And ours."

"But Sylvie has forgotten that part."

We were interrupted by Luc, who came to announce that dinner was ready. A giant onion frittata that Max praised to the high heavens, though with pedantic asides on just how he would have cooked it differently. Christine paid him no mind. And neither did we. The next day Natalija had an appointment with her hairdresser and all we cared about was making sure we arranged for the best possible surveillance.

"It's important that all of us be there," Beniamino hammered home. "We need to figure out whether or not the Garašanins intend to hold up their end of the deal."

"I'd be amazed if they didn't," I retorted. "We're holding their Uncle Lazar hostage and they are completely determined to get their hands on all of Dinić's businesses."

Rossini finished chewing a mouthful of food. "Never trust a bunch of Serbian gangsters, especially if you're not Serbian yourself," he pronounced. "For all we know, at this very moment, they're negotiating with Natalija because they've decided that an alliance would be more useful and don't care if Lazar does wind up in an unmarked grave."

I nodded but Beniamino clearly didn't think we were done with our discussion. "I don't understand why you trust Bojana."

That wasn't entirely true. Still, I'd taken the value of the hostage for granted. "I made a mistake," I admitted easily.

Rossini turned to the others. "Should we dig a little deeper?"

Max grinned. "That won't be necessary. The fact is that Marco's been mooning after a certain hot bartender and his brains have turned to mush."

"Well, who is she?" Luc and Christine wanted to know. The fat man didn't have to be asked twice. "She's an ex-porn star."

"If she's French, Luc is bound to know her work," Christine broke in. "He's a compulsive consumer of pornos."

"Not true. I like erotic movies. And what's wrong with that?" her husband said, putting up a lame defense.

"If you ask me, they're boring," added his spouse. "Right?" Beniamino, Max, and I voiced our agreement.

"You've just handed me over to the enemy," Luc said, giving us a look of reproof. "From now on, my life is going to be a living hell. I'm going to be put on a diet of heist flicks. That's all Christine will watch."

We all broke out laughing and went on ribbing him for a good long while. But our friend Christine hadn't missed the point that I still hadn't revealed the name of my bartender.

When I told them the name she went by professionally, Luc's eyes widened in surprise. "Wow, she's gorgeous."

"Yes. The most beautiful woman on earth," I sighed.

I caught the mocking, baffled glances my friends were exchanging and insisted that what I was telling them was nothing but the honest truth. "And I'll never forget her."

"I can't believe it," Rossini blurted out in amazement. "You've gone all gooey again over some woman who doesn't even want you."

"Who didn't understand me," I corrected him. "That's a different matter."

"*Spudorato bugiardo*," Christine scolded me in Italian, calling me a shameless liar as she refilled my glass.

Alarm clock at six A.M. Coffee and dry biscuits. Then back into the train, packed in with commuters and students. It was raining, for a change. A fine, irritating drizzle. We bought umbrellas from a young man from Ghana who was slightly offended when we didn't try to haggle over the price.

"It's not because you think I'm a starving beggar and you're just trying to give me charity, is it?" he asked.

"No," Max replied. "We're just in a hurry. No matter what, your price is too high."

"Your fault," the young man shot back. "I would have been glad to knock the price on each item down fifty cents."

We spent the morning watching apartment building doors and doormen, streets and alleys, cars and public conveyances, faces, uniforms, restaurants, bars, and shops. As Max and I expected, Rossini chose the little garden courtyard in front of the building with the dentist's office.

"It's like a cage. Once she sets foot in there, she won't be able to get away," he said in a flat voice. He jutted his chin to point out the escape route. "We'll use a motorcycle. Luc'll drive."

"And you'll be on the opposite side of the street on another bike," he added, to Christine this time. "You'll be keeping an eye on the two bodyguards and any cops who happen along. If anyone pulls a gun, so do you."

We ate lunch separately. Max dragged me to rue de Brest, of course, where he methodically crammed himself full of food after studying the menu as if it were sacred scripture. He also ordered a number of dishes for me so that he could sample them himself. An extended tasting menu.

We caught up with the others not far from the hairdresser's an hour before Natalija's appointment, to make sure that Bojana hadn't invited us to a bloodbath. Everything looked quiet. We chose the glass window of a coffee shop as our vantage point. Natalija Dinić's car pulled up right on time. Bojana got out and opened the rear door and from the car emerged . . . Sylvie. From fifty yards away, the two women, the two great rivals, were identical. Rossini had turned to stone; he was white as a sheet.

He turned to look at us. "Her hair," he stammered in a hoarse voice. "Sylvie has been wearing hers like that for a little over a month. How could she know that? And the coat? It's a Marras from last year, I gave it to her at the beginning of March, and Sylvie can't have worn it more than two or three times."

"Someone has been spying on her," I whispered, my stomach churning at the implications of that fact.

Natalija was still a few steps ahead of us. She knew that Sylvie was in Beirut, and if she knew about her style preferences and the recent changes to her apperance, that meant that Natalija was close enough to kill her whenever she chose. Or, worse, kidnap her again.

"I never suspected a thing," Rossini admitted, in horror. "I thought I'd put my wife somewhere safe, but I couldn't have been more wrong."

Just then Ana, the Serbian gangster's second bodyguard, got out of the car and leaned on the door. Bojana went over to her and together they started scanning the street circumspectly. It only took them a few seconds to spot us. Bojana Garašanin started in our direction and strolled past the window with a quizzical look on her face. Rossini shook his head to reassure her that nothing would happen that day.

The moment had come to vacate the premises, but Beniamino was still glued to his seat.

"I want to get a good look at her. I want to understand how close the resemblance is."

And so we waited, surrounded by faux cappuccinos and slices of too-sweet cake. The two bodyguards couldn't figure out what we were still doing there. They talked intently the whole time, wrapped in ankle-length down coats loose enough to effortlessly conceal the weapons they wore on their belts.

Bojana took out her cell phone and a second later mine started ringing.

"Should I be worried?" she asked.

"No," I replied. "The resemblance is stunning and we're just trying to come to terms with this insanity."

"Understood. Have you made up your minds about when you're going to act? The clock is ticking and she might sniff out the danger."

"Soon. Very soon," I replied. I didn't hang up right away. I couldn't miss this opportunity to ask a very specific question. "Does your boss know where Sylvie is hiding?"

"It seems to me I was pretty clear when I told you that she studies her photographs continuously. They come by email a couple of times a month. And the two Druze guarding her are just a couple of old jerks," she explained, and then hung up.

To see Natalija Dinić again was even more stunning.

She emerged from the doorway walking just as Sylvie did; her face bore the same fierce expression as the Franco-Algerian dancer's so often had when I'd admired it, thousands of times in the past. Only she was the wrong person. Unlike Rossini's woman, she was rotten inside. Pitiless, cruel, and perverse. Dangerous.

At the sight of our stunned reactions, Christine Duriez reacted sternly. "Wipe those stupid expressions off your faces," she hissed. "It's nothing but a crude replica."

A few hours later, at the end of a silent dinner, I informed the others that Bojana had calmly admitted that someone had been spying on Sylvie in Beirut.

"She's always been able to rely on powerful connections," said Beniamino. "But the thing I don't get is how the Garašanins are going to justify her death and take over her businesses. Bojana is one of them, everyone will think it's strange that she failed to lift a finger to protect her boss."

Suddenly I glimpsed the whole matter from a completely different point of view. Beniamino had been right when he'd scolded me for the trust I'd placed in Bojana. "She and Ana are going to open fire the second after you kill Dinić."

"Probably. They're going to use the fact that we consider them our accomplices to shoot me when I least expect it. Her willingness to cooperate just helps to create an atmosphere of trust, to get me to lower my guard."

"We're forgetting about Lazar," Max broke in.

"No, we're not," I retorted. "Their objective is to eliminate the threat that Beniamino constitutes. They'll pretend to offer the two of us safety in exchange for their uncle."

"It was the way they acted today that put me back on my guard," Rossini explained. "They stood there the whole time leaning against the car in the bitter cold, instead of taking advantage of those comfortable leather seats. Ready to open fire."

"So what are we going to do?" Luc asked.

Rossini stood up and got a bowl full of walnuts and a bottle of wine from the sideboard. "We'll change the plan," he replied.

"We can't kill Bojana," I hastened to remind him. "That would mean declaring war on the Garašanin family."

"And we can't afford that," Rossini added. "If we can't think of a way to screw them all, we'll have to think about just setting Lazar free and escaping to the far side of the planet with Sylvie."

"South America," suggested Christine.

"Australia," Luc proposed as an alternative.

Max and I looked at each other, appalled, and immediately started racking our brains for an idea.

An execution in the middle of a large city like Lyon was a damned serious matter. The police exercised minute and extensive control over the city, and the all but certain firefight with the two Serbian women further complicated things. If we wanted to have a decent chance of coming out of this alive and free, we'd need the time to do thorough advance work. Instead, we'd only had one night to patch together a plan, a single violent blow based on the desperate awareness that Natalija was stronger than us and that we absolutely had to kill her that same day.

After Luc, Christine, and Beniamino roared away aboard a pair of high-powered motorbikes that they'd stolen from the chop shop where they'd been stored until just moments before, I started running down the long list of unknowns that could undermine the outcome of the operation. Most of them seemed to have something to do with me.

"You drive," I told Max, tossing him the car keys. "The way I feel right now, I might hit someone."

The fat man gave me a sour look.

"Don't worry, when the time comes I'll be perfectly calm and everything will go off without a hitch," I retorted irritably.

When I reached my position, old Rossini was just entering the little garden. He was wearing a long raincoat over his motorcycle jacket and he'd perched a flat cap white as snow on his head. Details that any eyewitnesses would remember accurately, forgetting the other details that might actually have helped to identify him. Immediately afterward he vanished, tucked away into a providential recess in the apartment building's façade. Another ten minutes and darkness would fall. Exactly when we expected our target to show up.

In that kind of situation, time runs exasperatingly slow. I felt like I was about to lose my mind, and I couldn't seem to sit still. Luc and Christine, on the other hand, were ostentatiously relaxed. No one would ever have guessed that they were both armed and ready to shoot at a moment's notice.

At last the car pulled up. Just as she had the day before, Bojana got out and opened the rear door. At that exact moment, I pulled out my cell phone and called her, praying that her phone would be on and that the gods of mobile telephony would look down kindly upon me.

She answered on the second ring, just as she was helping Natalija out of the car. "A sniper has Ana in his sights," I lied, hoping I sounded convincing. "She's a dead woman if you try to screw us. It's in your interest to get out of here fast."

The Serbian bodyguard snapped her phone shut. Her eyes scoured the street trying to spot me. I raised one hand to make it easier for her.

Bojana walked her boss to the gate leading into the little garden and then went back to the car. A few seconds later, Ana started the engine back up and took off, tires screeching.

Dinić whipped around. She realized that she'd just been betrayed and accelerated her pace, hoping to find safety inside. But Rossini blocked her way, leveling a pistol fitted with a silencer straight at her chest.

Natalija smiled and threw her arms wide. "My love," she exclaimed and hugged him tight, whispering tender words. The same words that Sylvie would have used, a mixture of Arabic and French.

The old bandit collapsed under the weight of the Serbian woman's umpteenth brilliant ploy. Not only was she identical to his wife, but she knew all the secrets of their relationship. He couldn't bring himself to pull the trigger. He couldn't even break free of that embrace.

It was Christine who finally put an end to the impasse. She raced across the street and, when she reached them, she placed the muzzle of the big-bore revolver against the woman's temple and fired. Natalija Dinić dropped to the ground. Beniamino went on staring at her, misty-eyed. His face was spattered with her blood. Christine grabbed him by the arm and forced him to start walking. But the old bandit moved slowly, awkwardly.

"You're going to get us killed like this," the bank robber from Marseille implored him. "We've got to get out of here fast."

At last, Rossini snapped out of it. "Yes, let's get out of here," he muttered and strode off with a brisk step toward Luc, who was waiting for him with the motor running. Christine put on her helmet and roared off a second later. People started to pour out of the Académie de Billard, attracted by the sounds of gunshots.

I walked away, doing my best to keep from breaking into a run. Max had parked in a nearby side street. He peppered me with questions when he found out that it had been our friend Christine who shot and killed Dinić. He couldn't believe that Beniamino could collapse like that either.

I called Bojana. She attacked me with a string of insults.

"Do you want to know where to go get Uncle Lazar or shall we talk again after you've calmed down?"

"There was no need to put Ana's life in danger," she retorted furiously.

"We couldn't trust you," I said, cutting her off. I gave her the address of the farmhouse. "He's locked in the basement."

"I just hope you treated him well. My family might not be pleased," the Serbian woman said in a threatening tone of voice.

"From this moment on, as far as all the members of the Garašanin family are concerned, we no longer exist," I stated, enunciating my words very clearly. "Otherwise we'll circulate the video that shows how Natalija Dinić was betrayed by her bodyguards."

Bojana said nothing. Then she hung up. I was sure we'd never see her again.

"You've gotten so good at spinning bullshit," Max said, admiringly.

I broke the phone's SIM card in half and tossed it out the car window. A gust of icy wind blew in.

"Let's just hope this is all over," I sighed.

The fat man said nothing. He handed me a flask of Calvados. An act of brotherly kindness. It was exactly what I needed.

There was no one at the safe house but the couple from Marseille.

"Beniamino decided to stay in Vienne," Luc explained. "He said he needed some time alone."

Christine finished rolling herself a cigarette. "I don't like the fact that he's driving around on a stolen motorcycle that was used in a murder. Natalija Dinić was a big gun and all the cops in town are going to have their eyes peeled."

"He ought to be here, safe, with us," her husband chimed in.

"I'll go find him," I said.

I found him sitting on the steps of a small Roman temple in a city square. He was smoking a cigarette and drinking a beer. It was really too cold to brave the out-of-doors, but plenty of other patrons of the bar that had served Beniamino were sitting outside so they could enjoy a cigarette.

I joined him, though I couldn't keep from expressing a note of disapproval.

"How the fuck are you sitting on this goddamned ice-cold piece of stone?"

"Your ass is resting on a piece of history. Try to show some respect."

I nodded and looked around for the motorcycle.

"I hid it," he reassured me. "They'll find it come spring-time."

"Luc and Christine are worried. And so are we."

"Did you think I'd gone nuts and forgotten the basic rules for a killer on the run?"

The bitterness of his tone couldn't conceal the despair in his voice.

"What happened?"

He took a sip and handed me the glass. "Natalija was a creature straight from hell," he explained. "She was happy to see me. She wasn't afraid of my gun, much less the look of hatred in my eyes. She embraced me and whispered words of love in my ear. The same exact words that Sylvie used. Her voice was identical, even the way she caressed my back was the same. For a long moment I believed that she was my woman. I'm just lucky that Christine took care of wiping her off the face of the earth."

"We've always been puppets dancing on Dinić's string." I'd been wanting to talk about this for a while, and now was the time. "Maybe because she was a woman, maybe because she was a clone of Sylvie, but we've never been clear-eyed and determined in our fight against her."

"What do you mean?"

"Twice now you've aimed a gun straight at her, and both times you failed to pull the trigger."

"The first time it was Sylvie who asked me to kill only her husband."

"And you knew perfectly well that killing her man at the altar as the two of them were swearing their undying love in the presence of a patriarch would inevitably lead to all this. We could have spared ourselves years of pointless suffering."

He sighed. "You're right. What do you want me to do? Say I'm sorry?"

I grabbed his arm and squeezed it hard. "Don't even think of it. But now you get back to Sylvie and do your best to make things right."

"First we're going to have to make a withdrawal. We're out of money, Marco."

"Whose turn is it this time?"

"A jeweler in Avignon. The proprietor is a fence and a police informer."

I snorted. "He deserves it but that doesn't make it any less dangerous," I said as I stood up. "I can't take this cold anymore. And I'm hungry."

"Who do you think has the run of the kitchen this time, Max or Christine?"

"I'd bet on the woman from Marseille."

I would have won, too. With a clean apron and a pair of oven mitts she hardly seemed like the woman who just a few hours earlier had eliminated one of the unquestioned queens of the Serbian criminal underworld.

A pork roast and baked potatoes with sour cream. Rossini waited until the food and the red wine had to some extent alleviated the tension that had built up; then he thanked Christine. "I'll always be grateful to you for what you did."

She stood up and planted a kiss on his forehead. "It was a real pleasure to murder that slut."

Beniamino wrapped her in an affectionate embrace. "I'd still be standing there in a daze, with no idea what to do," he confided without embarrassment.

Luc raised a glass. "Here's to victory, and to the end of this war."

Max followed suit. "Here's to Sylvie, and here's to all of us."

The following morning our tiny army broke ranks. There was no longer any reason for it to exist. Beniamino and the couple from Marseille left for Avignon by train, Max went back to Italy, and I headed for Ninon.

I was almost certain that she'd give me the heave-ho but I needed to be with a woman, I needed to share a little affection with someone, share the routine of everyday life.

When I walked into the Tip Top Bar she was talking with a supplier and pretended not to notice me. The two regular customers greeted me with sympathetic smiles. I sat down and started leafing through a sports paper, waiting for the moment to approach the bar and receive the harsh treatment I certainly deserved.

At a certain point I realized that she was staring at me, her lips twisted into a sneer of contempt. I steeled myself and stood up.

"*Ciao,* Ninon."

"What are you doing here?"

"I need a little advice," I said, taking a stab in the dark. "It's too cold out to go on drinking beer and anisette boilermakers. I'd like an alternative that'll heat me up just right."

"Am I supposed to find that bullshit you just served up somehow interesting?"

"I'm surprised. It struck me as a brilliant pickup line. Concise and amusing, in other words just perfect."

"What do you want?"

"To stay with you," I replied, serious now. "For a while. As long as you want. A minute or the rest of my life."

"There've been two others in the meanwhile," she informed me in a hard voice.

I shrugged. "I'll manage to survive that piece of news," I shot back playfully, even if I'd have preferred never to know.

"I like you but you've turned out to be a real disappointment."

"I'll behave."

She stuck her hand in her bucket purse, rummaging around for her house keys. "I don't want you here, upholstering my bar," she clarified, before handing me the keys. "I'll see you tonight."

I left the bar feeling like a man who had just been healed by a miracle, and suddenly regained the use of his legs. She came in late that night, got comfortable next to me on the big sofa in front of the television set. We watched a couple of episodes of a show in which mankind does its best to survive a zombie apocalypse. She fell asleep with her head on my chest.

We started having sex again after a few days. We were in no hurry and neither of us was looking to prove anything. We were two people who'd decided to keep each other company for a while.

The one day the bar was closed, I squired her around town. A little shopping, a few museum exhibits, the movies, and an Indian restaurant or two: these were the things she loved. I tried to take her to a blues concert but she vetoed that idea firmly.

"You'd have to be a missionary or a Red Cross volunteer to want to listen to music born out of slavery. Sadder than hell."

I disagreed and time was I would have argued the point with deranged fury; but just then, I found the way she said it absolutely irresistible.

Ninon liked novels. She had a friend with a bookstore, and she'd pick out books for Ninon and drop them off at the bar. She'd spend her mornings reading. After breakfast she went back to bed and hungrily devoured page after page.

I had plenty of time to myself and every once in a while I'd play a DVD from her career as a porn star. Men with overgrown cocks, women too horny to be true, and threadbare plots. Ninon was the most beautiful actress, and her husband the actor most generously endowed by Mother Nature.

It made a strange impression on me to watch her. It didn't turn me on, but I didn't dislike it either. One day she asked me a very specific question, taking it for granted that I'd watched her movies.

"I know your artistic opus by heart but I don't recognize you, I don't smell the scent of your skin. In short, I see the actress."

"Does it bother you that I've worked in the porn industry?"

"Not a bit," I replied, stung.

"Then stop keeping a safe distance between your dick and my ass."

That's just the way Ninon was.

One day Rossini came to see me. We met in a restaurant about ten kilometers outside of town.

"I'm leaving for Beirut," he announced. "I'm going to see the one I love."

"How is she?"

"The same," he replied, pulling a fat manila envelope out of his inside jacket pocket. It was full of cash.

"That's a lot of money," I observed. "I don't need that much."

"Everyone always needs money," he retorted. "And the job came off nicely. The kind of job that sets you up for a nice long time."

"News about the Garašanins?"

"Bojana has been punished. The family called her back to Belgrade, but without her girlfriend Ana, who has apparently been sent to run a drug-dealing network in Hamburg."

"Solid source?"

"Solid and certified. I've bought more than a few pieces off Vukašin Joksimovič."

Joksimovič was a notorious Serbian arms dealer, an independent operator who supplied anyone who came along, without getting permission from the various mafia families. He had a sincere liking for old Rossini and would never give him bad intelligence.

"That was cruel of them. There was no need to mess with her emotional life," I commented.

"If Bojana wasn't the daughter of one of the bosses, she'd be six feet under by now. Ana's going to have to pay the price for the two of them, and I'd be willing to bet that a few months from now she'll be behind bars, serving time for trafficking in narcotics."

"They can go fuck themselves," I said, cutting the discussion short and moving on to more agreeable topics.

"Did I already tell you that her name is Ninon?"

"The porn star? Yes."

"She used to be," I clarified for no real reason. "In any case, for once I'm happy. I take care of unimportant details so that I can live comfortably with her. And I'm satisfied with that. The gang war drained me, and I'm having a hard time getting back into gear."

"Will it last?"

I shook my head. "No. It's just an interlude."

"Or else it's a limbo . . ."

"Whatever it is, it works for me."

Time flowed over our lives and we didn't even notice. I lived at Ninon's place for more than two years and it was actually Beniamino who finally dragged me away. Looking back after all this time I can admit that I was happy with that woman. She'd figured out that our castle was bound to crumble the minute she started asking questions, and in fact she was careful not to ask them. As for me, I'd taken great care not to oppress her with what she referred to as "the usual bullshit I get from men."

We'd spend hours at a time in silence, but every time we happened to catch each other's eyes, we would smile. Tender, vulnerable, but real. Back then, the money from Rossini allowed me to do nothing at all. I'd started getting back into the blues with a certain focus. I read articles and books, I bought records, I went out to hear French and American musicians passing through. And I had the good luck of hearing at the last minute about a concert by the great singer and harmonica player Fabrizio Poggi who was performing with his band Chicken Mambo. His version of *I'm On the Road Again* warmed my heart. But it didn't always go that way. Sometimes I'd come home upset. The blues can be cruel; without you even noticing, the blues will dig a hole inside you, will slap you in the face with memories, or push you into a pit of nostalgia.

But as always, the blues fed my sense of equilibrium.

My relationship with alcohol had changed, too. I drank less than I used to. A glass always seemed to last longer. Ninon was good for me, she seemed to limit the excesses that I required to tolerate life.

The phone call came late one spring afternoon. I'd followed the twists and turns of a mountain road all the way up to a tiny village where a group of ex-hippies lived. With the passing of the years, they'd come to appreciate the importance of organic farming and started producing first-class wines and cheeses.

I was spreading a blue-veined goat cheese onto half a baguette when my cell phone started buzzing in my shirt pocket.

"You need to come to Beirut," said Rossini, sad and worried. I knew that tone of voice, and this was no time to ask questions.

"All right."

"You'll get a call from Max, he's organizing your trip."

Two minutes later, the fat man called. "What's happening?" I asked.

"No idea. Beniamino didn't tell me. We'll find out when we get to Lebanon."

I wasn't at all happy to hear from my friends that day and in that way. I had no desire to leave my Ninon, and I knew that if I wanted to keep from lying to her, I'd have to stick her with a line something like: "I have to leave, I can't tell you why, and I don't know if and when I'll ever come back."

When I did it, she looked at the duffel bag that now contained all my worldly possessions and pointed to the door. "Good luck," was all she said before closing the bedroom door behind her.

I slipped out of her life with a feeling of death in my heart. As I was driving straight to the airport, I did my best to justify my actions, telling myself that in the world I came from, when a friend calls you, nothing else really counts for much.

I landed at Charles de Gaulle airport, where Max was waiting for me. I found him at the duty-free shop as he was loading up on foie gras and French chocolates.

I gave him a hug. "I hadn't heard there was a famine in Lebanon."

"Always best to stock up, just in case," he retorted, showing me a bottle of Calvados.

We waited for our flight to be called in a nondescript bar disguised as a brasserie. The staff hated travelers passing through and treated them with a brazen and relentless rudeness.

Max was in the mood for a fight but I managed to calm him

down. "In all this time, neither one of us felt the urge to reach out to the other. Are we still friends?" I asked.

"What a bullshit question," he replied, pretending to be offended. "The truth is that you've been so clingy over the past few years that a little distance was necessary, therapeutic even."

"I almost never thought about you and I never missed you at all."

The fat man gave me a level stare with his pale blue eyes. "As far as that goes, I haven't exactly been wallowing in nostalgia either," he shot back, changing his tone of voice. "You want to play truth or dare? I'm happy to. That fucking gang war ruined our lives and we needed time and distance from everything that might remind us of what we'd been through. Even our dearest friends."

As he spoke, I sized him up attentively. He was tan, and even if he hadn't lost so much as an ounce, he was still looking pretty fit.

"What have you been doing all this time, Max?" I asked, my curiosity aroused.

"Are you already tired of playing the game?"

"Yes, just answer my question."

"I worked in an alpine hut in the mountains."

"So that's why you look like Friar Tuck from Robin Hood," I joked. "Didn't Beniamino set you up with some of the take from the robbery?"

"Of course he did. But I didn't spend much of it, in fact for once in my life I even managed to set a little something aside."

I leaned over the table. "What's happened to you?"

"Nothing. It's just that I didn't know where to go or what to do. I traveled around a little, hitting Padua, Venice, and Treviso, and then I lucked into this opportunity."

"A woman? A shrink with her office in a mountain hut?"

"No. A guy I knew from the university. He needed someone to help out in the kitchen."

"And how did you like it?"

"Just fine. In the winter I went a little further downhill and I set down roots in a small town in Cadore where there are fewer and fewer tourists every season and the ski lifts are just rusty souvenirs of the past . . ."

"That must have been a load of fun."

"Actually, it was," he replied, smiling. "A nice house, a fireplace, plenty of books, and a lady who likes men with a gut."

"But?"

"I miss the life we used to live, our investigations, my archives. Don't you?"

"I don't know, Max. Maybe. It also depends on what's waiting for us in Beirut. Until yesterday I was living with a woman I love."

"Your Ninon. Beniamino told me about it."

"You stayed in touch?" I asked, surprised.

"Every now and then."

"But you have no idea what's happened in Lebanon?"

"No. But I'm pretty sure that whatever it was, it'll kill our good moods for a while."

Waiting for us at the airport were Talal and Wiam, the two Druze who had until then been in charge of Sylvie's security. They greeted us courteously but they had changed since the first time we'd met them. They were curved, bent, as if they'd been carrying a heavy weight on their shoulders, their faces sliced by a bitter grimace as thin as a scar from a razor. I decided that old Rossini must have given them quite the going over after finding out that Natalija Dinić could have hit Sylvie at the time of her choosing. But too much time had gone by since then, and they still had their jobs. So it had to be something else.

Max tried to pry a little information out of them, but they both pretended not to understand French anymore.

Sylvie lived in a beautiful three-story beach house overlooking an ugly beach. But the views of the city and of the water were enchanting. The building dated from the sixties and the landlord had decorated it somewhat eccentrically. There were lots of paintings hanging on the walls but not a single photograph. And the framed paintings depicted landscapes completely devoid of human beings.

Beniamino welcomed us in the big living room, sitting in an armchair. He didn't get up to greet us. He pointed us to the couch.

"Thanks for coming," he said in a low voice. "It wasn't me who asked you to come. It was Sylvie."

He couldn't bring himself to go on. He stood up and hurried over to grab a crystal pitcher and pour himself a glass of water. He gulped it down in the manner of someone who hadn't had a drink in some time.

"She's decided to take her life, and she wants to say good-bye to you."

Max the Memory's eyes filled with tears. I remained dry-eyed, but I had to call on all my self-control in order to keep from crying out in despair.

We sat in silence, drowning in grief. Our shared personal code kept us from appealing to any presumptive common sense, from grabbing Beniamino and crying out: "Stop her! Convince her to live!" From throwing ourselves at Sylvie's feet and imploring her.

In our world, a person was free, even to end her own life, and no one would ever claim the right to raise his voice in dissent. People's choices had to be respected, even if they made your heart and your brain bleed. Which is why it was the right thing to do: to announce your imminent suicide and leave this world surrounded by friends, because nothing could be worse than to say farewell in loneliness and secrecy out of the fear you might wind up in an institution. Our outlaw hearts were big enough; they could—they would—accept it.

"I'll go get her," Rossini muttered.

A short while later he returned, arm in arm with the woman he loved, the woman for whom he'd fought and suffered. Sylvie was beautiful, but I couldn't help remembering how Natalija Dinić had modified her own body to resemble her.

As usual, she kissed us each on both cheeks and on the forehead. She was strangely serene.

"From the looks on your faces I have to assume that Beniamino has already told you the news," she said in a calm voice. "I know that I don't have to explain the reasons behind my decision, but we've been friends for so many years that it seems only right to share my rationale with you.

"I'm sad to say that the wounds to my heart have never healed. I've been subjected to too much violence by too many people. I was raped, I was used as a plaything, I was tortured, forced to dance for mobs of men, after which they'd unleash their lust and anger on me like a herd of pigs.

"Nothing has been able to help me forget, not the endless love offered by Beniamino, not the finest medical therapies. Not even the passage of time. Life has become, now, intolerable. Only death is strong enough to sweep away this dull pain that hounds me even in my sleep. I need peace.

"Now that Natalija Dinić is dead and the gang war is over, there are no more obligations forcing me to go on living."

She smiled at us, gazing intently into our eyes. I wondered how long she'd been ready to put an end to the game that had been lost from the very beginning.

Wiam served the aperitifs with tears streaking his face. Sylvie, determined to break the wall of our sorrowful silence, forced us to chat. She asked me all about Ninon, and Max sang the praises of a beautiful winter in the mountains.

At the dinner table she asked whether we would be going back to the Veneto to live. But she didn't wait to hear the answer. "When I met Beniamino I was dancing in a nightclub in Oderzo and I was going around on a wonderful motorcycle. It's almost as if I can still feel the sharp winter air lashing my face," she remembered, a moment before setting her silverware down on her plate and throwing herself out the window.

The thud of her body hitting the white and blue tiles in the courtyard below was bloodcurdling.

I started to get up but Rossini shook his head, his face pale, his hands clutching the edge of the table. "Talal and Wiam will see to her body. Sylvie was very clear in her wishes," he said in a broken voice. "There will be no funeral, she wishes to be buried at sea, in the waters just off this villa. We can go now."

"She could still be alive, she might need our help," I hissed in a choking voice. "Beniamino, please."

"Cut it out, Marco. There's nothing we can do, and I feel as if I'm losing my mind."

An hour later we were studying the departures board for the first flight that would take us away from Beirut once and for all. I was engulfed by a surging tide of sensations and having a hard time getting a grip on reality. My outlaw heart couldn't seem to come to terms with the death of a person so dear to me, a person who had stood up right in the middle of dinner and jumped out the window. I lost sight of Max and Beniamino and found myself on a flight to Rome, where I would connect to another flight that would take me to Cagliari, Sardinia. The temptation to go back to Ninon had been powerful, almost overwhelmingly so, but I wasn't enough of a bastard to use her to work through my feelings of grief and defeat. In the end, Natalija Dinić had claimed her revenge.

While the customs agents were searching my luggage for the drugs that I couldn't possibly not be transporting, given that I was an ex-convict on my way back from Lebanon, I called Beniamino. I wanted to let him know how much I cared about him. He didn't pick up.

CHAPTER TWO

I was staying in a three-star hotel that deserved no more than two, in a narrow, ancient alley in the Marina quarter. Breakfast time was long past and I had to settle for an espresso. The proprietor's mother-in-law was subjecting me, as she did every morning, to a rapid-fire burst of questions about my private life, to which I didn't bother to respond. She had figured out that I was a good for nothing and wanted to prove the fact to that idiot son-in-law of hers.

Her convictions about me suddenly began to vacillate when she saw a refined and elegantly attired lady walk in and head in my direction.

"I decided it might be better to move our appointment up to lunchtime," the Swiss woman said, skipping right over the conventional hellos.

"How did you find me?"

"Giannella took care of it. She got the address from a certain . . ."

"Max," I said, finishing her sentence for her while I wondered why the fat man was scheming to get me to talk to that woman at all costs.

"I don't understand why Counselor Marzolo doesn't bother to protect my privacy," I complained. "I think I may have to get a new lawyer."

"I'm sure she'll be able to handle the disappointment. Shall we go?"

I looked at my watch. "But it's not even noon yet. Signora,

this is Cagliari, no one is going to serve us lunch at this time of day."

The shrew at the reception desk snickered audibly, and I took advantage of the opportunity to suggest renewing our evening appointment, an appointment I didn't have the slightest intention of keeping. But the lady must have smelled a rat and she insisted on an aperitif and lunch.

"All right," I said, giving in. "But first I need to make a phone call."

I went off to a small side room and called Max. I hadn't talked to him since the night Sylvie had decided to end her life.

"Where are you now?" I asked.

"Back in the alpine hut."

"Why did you send that intolerable woman after me?"

"Because Sylvie is dead, Natalija is dead, and that whole story is dead and buried."

"And so?"

"Now we can . . . now we *must* go back to our old lives."

"This sounds like an argument a married couple might have, and you and I aren't one, Max. Plus we've said this too many times, too recently, and it's never worked."

"Let's start the old business back up. It's the only thing we know how to do."

"Times have changed and we're out of the game. We don't even have a house in Padua anymore."

He started shouting. "What the fuck's wrong with you? Why won't you listen to me? I can't take it anymore, don't you get it? I'm falling apart."

I raised my voice in response. "I've already fallen apart! I don't know why I don't just drink myself to death."

My friend fell silent for a long time, and then asked: "Do you mean that?"

I sighed. "No. I'm just at the end of my rope. The sound of

Sylvie's body hitting the tiles in the courtyard keeps ringing in my ears and I can't get it out of my mind."

"I was there that night too."

It was my turn to fall silent.

"I'm begging you, listen to what the Swiss woman has to say and then call me back," the fat man suggested.

"Max, I can't think clearly."

"I'm begging you."

"Okay."

I found myself sitting at a small table in a café, sipping a Canossian Sister and stuffing my mouth with salted peanuts. The lady didn't seem able to make up her mind. Neither to drink nor to tell her story.

"I'm listening," I said.

"And I'm waiting for you to stop gorging yourself on cocktail nuts."

It occurred to me only she could have used the term "cocktail nuts." I rubbed my mouth with the back of my hand. "Excuse me, I skipped breakfast."

"You slept in, didn't you? Because you had too much to drink last night."

"That's my business."

"It's my business too, since I'm about to reveal the details of a rather delicate matter."

"Cut it out. Either you trust me or you might as well pick your ass up off that chair and hightail it back to Lugano."

"Don't be vulgar," she scolded me; but she remained in her seat. And she told me a story that was decidedly out of the ordinary. Even for an unlicensed private detective like yours truly.

Guido was running late. It was the first time, but I couldn't help my irritation. I made a mental note to upbraid him, even if it meant ruining the tryst that I'd yearned for and planned with such meticulous care. I have never been able to stand it when other people waste my time. Especially when it comes to sex. Absolutely unacceptable. The time that belongs to lovers is always stolen from lives built on other affections, passions, and routines. Structures that are at once exceedingly complex and yet so delicate that a clandestine affair can destroy them merely by announcing its existence.

I know a lot about this sort of thing. That's why I have caged my love for Guido, cordoned it off with a series of strict rules governing behavior and security. Foolproof. Because this is true love, and for that reason it deserves to live on in secret in our hearts. And yet, at the same time, we can hardly afford to lay waste our official lives. Guido has been engaged to Enrica forever and he loves her deeply. He never pretended for even an instant that I, his mistress, could hope to be the sole and single recipient of his love. Guido loves us in two completely different ways, but nothing on earth could persuade him to leave Enrica.

I, on the other hand, fell out of love with my husband a long time ago, but that's just the luck of the draw in married life. Ugo is a mediocre man in terms of human qualities, but he's a genius at business. I only realized that after the birth of Ilaria, too late to retrace my steps and give up a quiet, comfortable life in the midst of Massagno, just outside of Lugano.

Ilaria resembled her father more and more as she grew up, but at least she had the delicacy to pretend she cared about the feelings of others, especially those of her mother. Duty and decency require that she not ignore me entirely.

I can't say that I've been unhappy all my life. I was born and raised in a setting where relations between people aren't necessarily governed by feeling. The important thing is to maintain a state of harmony based on a healthy hypocrisy and intelligently calibrated lies. I assure you that the quality of life remains intact all the same. Money is an extraordinary resource when it comes to ensuring that everything is reasonably pleasant. I've never believed in the fairy tale of the wealthy young woman who abandons her family to live happily ever after with a woodsman or a worker on the assembly line. In boarding school, we used to tell those stories as if they were hilarious jokes, and none of the girls laughed harder than I did.

Believe me, it's no easy matter to be wealthy while keeping your emotions at bay. It takes an inner discipline that springs from steely daily practice, because at times you're tempted to believe that money is powerful enough to allow you to operate outside the bounds of social mores and customs. And that's a fatal error, one that can lead you to lose everything. When I say everything, I mean money.

I was certain that I was safe from all temptation until the day I met Guido. I'd boarded a train in Bologna and he was sitting in the seat across from me. We were both going to Venice. I had an appointment with an art dealer who wanted me to purchase several portraits from the 1930s. Guido, on the other hand, was going to the university to deliver a lecture. He's an assistant professor, an expert on literature. I'd pulled a novel out of my bag and, suddenly, he took it gently from my hands, begging my forgiveness and hastening to explain that he didn't want to bother me, but that he felt duty-bound to explain the reasons why he felt I should immediately stop reading that book.

At first I was almost put out by his intrusion, but then I'd never met a man like him before and I was immediately intrigued. A refined intellectual, with the exquisite manners of the nineteenth century, amiable and ironic. A good man. Harmless. Which men so rarely are.

It was an agreeable trip. I enjoyed his presence as an unexpected gift, a breath of fresh air. And I imagined nothing more, it didn't move beyond the bounds of fantasy. Not merely because that wasn't something I was accustomed to do, but especially because he was younger than me. By ten years, I later learned.

Guido was born in 1975. And I was certain that only men found it natural to dedicate themselves to younger women without a twinge of shame. I've always chosen my lovers from among men of my own age and have always felt contempt for women who take men young enough to be their sons, or just slightly older, to bed.

I soon learned that Guido was a connoisseur of painting as well. He gave me some advice about the artists I'd mentioned to him when I explained the reason for my Venetian interlude.

We said farewell at the station with a handshake and a friendly smile. But by the time I'd turned and taken ten steps, he was already just a memory.

A few hours later I chanced to see him again. I was chatting with the art dealer when I glimpsed him peeking through one of the gallery windows. He smiled when he caught my eye. I thought it would be nice to invite him in. He immediately confessed that he hadn't happened on me by chance. His curiosity had been piqued by my mention of the paintings and he wanted to see a few of them. The proprietor introduced himself and that was when I heard his name for the very first time. Guido Di Lello. He turned toward me with an outstretched hand and apologized for failing to introduce himself earlier on the train. "Oriana Pozzi Vitali," I said, enunciating clearly, as my family's prominence demanded.

Usually people immediately connect the double surname to my husband's companies. But he didn't. His world had nothing in common with mine.

I was uneasy. I'd never have expected him to come after me. Guido immediately hit it off with the art dealer, praising the selection of paintings that he was proposing I purchase.

I wanted to close the deal that same evening, but his presence was keeping me from doing so. I tactfully tried to make him understand that I would have preferred for him to leave. Never discuss money in front of strangers. Not only is it in poor taste, but it would have obliged me to show an aspect of my personality that I preferred to keep hidden because money should be spent, not wasted. Investing in art means paying as little as possible, especially when the economy is flagging. The dealer knew that I was going to drive a hard bargain and, when it became clear that the stranger wasn't going to get out from underfoot, he spared me any further embarrassment by suggesting we talk again the next day by phone.

Guido, who at that point was still just Professor Di Lello to me, asked whether I was headed for the station or whether I was planning to stay the night, in which case he would be exceptionally pleased to invite me to dinner.

I replied that we weren't sufficiently close for him to dare ask me such questions. He said that he agreed. He muttered an embarrassed farewell and turned to go, but before he'd taken three steps he turned back to ask my forgiveness. I've never met anyone as talented as he when it comes to slipping talk of unrelated matters between an excuse and an apology. He freely ransacked the archives of literature, proving to me with a slew of poetic citations that there was absolutely no harm in his desire to get to know me better. He anticipated every objection I might have raised, first and foremost the question of whether or not I might be interested in him as a person.

Five minutes. Not a minute more. And I surrendered. I was flattered that a professor in his mid-thirties, instead of chasing after co-eds, promising them good grades, should choose to court me. But I was also uncomfortable because I'd never before had a relationship with a man who lacked all familiarity with those material considerations against which I measured my very existence.

He insisted we go to a restaurant that a couple of his colleagues had recommended to him. I was sufficiently familiar with Venice to know that the place was nothing special. The chef was a trattoria cook who had renovated the place and then started wearing an immaculate chef's uniform, and the wine list was frankly abysmal. But I thought it would be tactless for me to point this out and I told him I would be delighted to go.

Guido had understood me to be a woman who cares about tra-

dition, etiquette, and that old-fashioned formality that is nothing other than a shell of armor that protects you from other people. He forced me to yield by making me laugh. Jokes, anecdotes, funny stories. Refined ones, obviously, nothing vulgar. I never heard a dirty word slip out of Guido's lips, not even one of those that has by now entered the common parlance.

When I realized that I desired him, a sense of fair play and sound reason demanded that I point out that I was older than him. That was an unpleasant interlude that dissolved in a split second the amusing atmosphere that had prevailed all evening.

Guido took my hand and confessed with disarming sincerity that I represented the pinnacle of his fantasies. That I was perfect.

I suddenly leapt to my feet and rushed to the restroom. And not out of embarrassment, but because of the excitement that those words had triggered in my mind. And in my body.

When I returned to the table I energetically played the part of the matron with a good head on her shoulders, pointing out that we had barely just met, hoping with all my heart that his answers to my objections would be persuasive enough to leave me with no avenue of escape.

All he had to do was reference a couple of novels. At that point I reasoned that even if we wanted to, and the desire was all too evident, we wouldn't be able to spend the night together because we certainly couldn't register together in a hotel. Certainly not in mine, where I was a familiar guest.

Guido suggested we go to his, which wasn't much more than a glorified pensione. At night there was no desk clerk and therefore the guests were simply given keys to the front door.

I hesitated for a moment. I wasn't all that certain that I wanted to go to bed with a man in a dump. Sex, no matter what people say, isn't something you can just do any old place. But then and there I couldn't seem to find a way to bring this up and so, as silently as a pair of cat burglars, we slipped into an unspeakably bleak hotel room that was, fortunately, quite clean.

Guido was delicate and careful. I found myself nude, in his arms, and it was as if he'd known me forever. He knew how, he knew where . . .

When I fled at five in the morning, he was fast asleep. I didn't want to be found out and treated like a stowaway. I hurried back to my hotel and slipped into bed. Happily topsy-turvy. Guido phoned at nine. I thought I was going to faint when the reception desk called to say that a certain Di Lello wanted to speak to me on the phone. I treated him sternly and arranged to meet him in a café.

I told him in no uncertain terms that if he ever hoped to see me again he was going to have to learn some basic rules of secrecy. While I laid out the ground rules, the astonishment on his face shifted into a smirk that turned him a little ugly.

He nibbled at a croissant and sipped his cappuccino in absolute silence.

Finally he said that he understood my need for secrecy, but that what he wanted to talk about just then was us. An urgent need dictated by the sheer beauty of the night before. He sang the praises of my body and said a thousand other things, each of which left indelible traces deep in my heart.

My husband and the few lovers I'd allowed myself over the years seemed like mere primates compared with him. That morning, in that café, I fell in love. Love. True love.

In a couple of months I had set up our parallel lives as a pair of clandestine lovers. I chose the Veneto because we both had interests in Venice so our travels were amply justified. But we couldn't be seen together in that city because the risk of being noticed was too great. And so, making use of a rather complicated series of financial machinations, I bought an apartment in the center of Padua.

One year, six months, and eleven days of happiness. Until the day that Guido failed to keep an appointment. It was the very first time. The cell phone with a Swiss service provider that he'd given me for our communications was turned off.

Disappointed, wounded, and terribly annoyed, I decided to leave, but while I was waiting for my train, my cell phone rang. I recognized the number. It was Guido.

The voice, however, belonged to a stranger, who informed me that my lover was in their hands and that unless I "coughed up" three hundred thousand euros inside of a week, they were going to kill him.

He put Guido on the line; sobbing, Guido begged me to pay.

The situation was too absurd to be real. It had to be a prank in very poor taste, and I hung up.

The stranger called right back. He told me that he knew that I couldn't lay my hands on that kind of money in cash, otherwise my husband would find out about it. He'd be willing to settle for some portion of my jewelry. He described the items and I realized that he must have seen them in photographs published in newspapers and magazines. A ribbon-cutting at a shopping mall, a few weddings, art openings, and the usual social occasions where people put themselves on display.

I objected that Ugo would find out anyway. The man shot back that I'd have plenty of time to dream up an appropriate excuse and what mattered most was that I'd have Guido back. He ordered me to keep my phone turned on and said that he'd call back in a couple of days with the details of the exchange.

I got onto the train and found a seat, moving automatically. The blood ran so cold in my veins that I could barely move my arms and legs. By the time I got off the train in Milan I'd made an irrevocable decision. I turned off my cell phone. And I used three different trash cans to get rid of the parts.

None of it concerned me anymore. Guido must have made some mistakes and broken the rules I had imposed. He had only himself to blame . . .

You think you know people, but you can never really trust them completely. Perhaps my lover had debts, and he was in cahoots with someone to get my money.

In any case, one reason kept me from involving myself in any way. And that reason was my husband. If Ugo ever found out about what happened, he'd throw me out of the house, and I'd lose everything, including my daughter.

Turning to the police would have meant attracting the interest of the media. I'd wind up in the news and our beautiful love story would be transformed into a squalid affair, just sex and betrayal. Even my own family would repudiate me, and I'd be forced to flee Switzerland.

No. It made no sense to ruin my life just to save Guido. That is, if it even was an actual kidnapping.

I went back to Massagno and waited for Guido to turn up, a corpse in a ditch somewhere, once the deadline had passed. But more than anything, I feared the criminals might take revenge by publicizing my illicit love affair. Instead, nothing happened at all.

Professor Di Lello was officially reported a missing person. The Italian press talked about it at length and even now, more than a year later, every so often that show on the RAI brings the case back up. His fiancée, Enrica, can't seem to let it go. Nor can his family and his colleagues at the university. They can't figure out why he would have decided to abandon his loved ones and his profession. Police investigations have produced no results. They've only ascertained one fact, through security camera recordings: the man boarded a train from Rome and got off in Padua.

He'd told Enrica that he had to go to Venice to meet a few of his students, but there is no evidence that this appointment ever existed. And so the question that torments her is this: why Padua? Was he planning to meet someone?

The only one who knows the truth is me. Guido was kidnapped by one or more criminals who wanted to extort three hundred thousand euros' worth of jewels out of me. I had no alternative but to protect myself and remain silent. I lived the first few months in terror. Then, once I realized I was safe, I could no longer stave off the desire to know the truth. I have to know what happened to Guido. If he's still alive. I want to know the names of the criminals who've stormed into my life. I don't feel the slightest sense of guilt, but the anxiety is eating at me. I've started to punish myself, displaying a weakness that I've never had before, allowing others, and in particular Ugo, to take advantage of me.

I can't go on living like this, you understand? You have to help me, Signor Buratti. I'll pay you well. Extremely well. The first real lesson I've learned from all this is that you can never rely entirely on family wealth, life is full of surprises and personal assets that no one knows about are precious, fundamental. And now I possess them.

I hope I've been clear. If I could, I'd use threats to force you to carry out this investigation. I don't like you, I suspect you're a criminal no different from the ones who tried to blackmail me, but I trust Giannella blindly.

How much do you want as a retainer? I imagine that asking for an estimate is foreign to your professional ethics, but in any case, the hotel safe contains enough cash to satisfy even your wildest dreams.

"Your beloved Guido is dead. There's no point in continuing to use the present tense when you talk about him," was the first thing that came out of my mouth.

The Swiss woman glared at me, full of hatred. "How can you be so sure of that?"

"You know it perfectly well yourself. Or do you think that the gang that kidnapped him decided to adopt him?"

"It's unnecessary for you to be so unpleasant."

"Signora, you need help," I said. "You can't hold out for long like this; you'll collapse and no one will be able to save you then."

"You just think about doing your job."

"Fine, I'll take the case, but on one condition: that you agree to take care of yourself. Take a vacation, sign in to a nice clinic for rich people, and get back on your feet."

"Are you trying to blackmail me too, Signor Buratti?"

I huffed in annoyance. "Call Giannella and give me the phone."

"Don't you know how to be courteous and polite?"

I shook my head. "No, Oriana. Just get used to it."

She pulled out her cell phone, spoke in an undertone with her old classmate, and then finally I was able to hear her voice myself.

"*Ciao*, attorney."

"So now you've heard the story, eh?"

"I'm going to repeat to you what I've already told this woman: I'm willing to investigate on one condition only, that a qualified shrink assume responsibility for arranging to get her put away for a while. And you've got to guarantee that this will happen very quickly; tomorrow morning I'm going to put her on the first plane and the minute she's back in Lugano she has to start a cure."

"I'll see what I can do."

"No, you have to give me your word right now," I shot back sternly. "Don't you see that she's undergone a trauma so powerful that not even her wealthy, old-fashioned, bourgeois defenses are enough to keep everything under control? There are cracks in her mind and her heart, she's a ticking time bomb, and if we aren't careful she'll take us all down with her."

"All right. Let me talk to her now."

Once again the cell phone changed hands. I caught the waitress's eye for another aperitif. And another bowl of peanuts. That day I would gladly have eaten a bucketful.

About twenty minutes later she returned to her seat. Her shoulders were slumped. "I'm not crazy, Signor Buratti."

"Of course you're not. You just need a complete overhaul."

"There is a note of hostility in your voice. Do you judge me for the way I behaved with Guido?"

"I have my opinions on the subject," I replied. "But you're

a client and I'll keep them to myself. As you can see, I'm even pretending not to be offended by your insults."

"Then why did you accept?"

"Because two people who are secretly in love should be left alone. Instead, a man was kidnapped and murdered and the woman he loved has been blackmailed. In my world, these crimes are unacceptable, but that's something you wouldn't understand."

"No," she admitted. "And to tell the truth, the circles you move in don't interest me. They only scare me."

I thought to myself that I'd never encountered a bigger bitch in my life. I moved onto practical details. "Does the apartment in Padua still belong to you?"

"Let's just say that I still have access to it."

"Fine, and now I have access to it. And I'd say that fifty thousand euros would be an acceptable down payment."

"Actually, I was thinking of a smaller sum."

"And you were wrong. Another fifty thousand if I solve the case. Plus expenses, obviously."

She stood up. "I'm tired, I'm going to get some rest. Tonight at dinner, I'll give you the money and the keys. I always have them with me, in case Guido comes back and wants to see me."

I paid the check and started walking back to my hotel. What I'd told the Swiss woman was only a half-truth. The real reason that was driving me to hunt down this gang of kidnappers was that it would keep my mind off my own problems for who knows how long. And the same went for Max. Investigating means starting down a tunnel where the darkness keeps you from looking around. Figuring out the truth about things that had nothing to do with me was a remedy for the emotional collapse I'd slid into after Sylvie's suicide. Actually, it had always been this way. From the first case I'd taken after getting out of prison. The problem was that I was accumulating stories I'd have to settle accounts with someday, when the past decided that those bills had come due. Just not today, and not tomorrow either. Before then, I needed to solve the mysterious disappearance of Professor Di Lello.

I phoned the fat man. "We have a client," I began.

"Partners again," he said promptly, making no secret of his relief. "Is it routine or an ugly mess?"

"It's a gigantic ugly mess. Nasty and foul."

"What kind of trouble has the lady gotten herself into?"

"You can't even begin to imagine. I'll tell you all about it when I get there, tomorrow or the day after, at the latest."

"Marco . . ."

"Yes?"

"Thanks."

"For what? Before I called you I was just thinking that we needed something to take our minds off our nightmares. And luck stepped in. That's all."

I stopped in a Chinese-run shop and bought a pen and a notepad. While I was paying for it, I ripped off the cover. It had a picture of such a sad-looking panda that it made you imagine all sorts of mistreatment.

I wasn't in the habit of taking notes. That smacked of TV detectives; but Oriana wasn't going to be around in the near future and I needed to be sure I was familiar with all the details.

Stretched out on the bed, I started jotting down the most important questions but by the time I got to the eleventh, I'd nodded off.

I woke up to the ringing of the phone in the room. The shrew informed me that Signora Pozzi Vitali would be expecting me at 8 P.M. at the restaurant Lo Zodiaco on Via Sassari.

"She was very clear: be on time!" she told me, before slamming down the receiver.

I showed up twenty minutes late. I hadn't done it on purpose. I'd just lingered too long in the shower. The signora was turning a glass of white wine slowly in her hands with an absent expression. As I sat down I noticed she was sweaty: the hair at her temples was matted down.

"Hot out this evening, isn't it?" I said. "Luckily, there's a breath of fresh air out here in the garden."

"Well, if nothing else it's not raining," she retorted in a flat voice. "This summer it's done nothing but rain in Lugano, and lakes and rain don't go very well together."

"It's true, it's a little depressing. When it's sunny, it's quite another matter."

"Right. So can we say we're done with chitchat and move on to more serious matters?"

"Perhaps we could order first, what do you say?"

"You have quite an appetite, for an alcoholic."

"I've gone to the very edge more than once but I've always managed to pull myself back just in time," I explained agreeably. "When I'm in love I drink less. Right now I'm not emotionally involved so I'm drinking more than usual, but hardly to excess."

"I can't imagine what kind of woman would be involved with someone like you." She waved her hand to take in the other tables. "Do you see any specimens here that might illuminate me?"

"Appearance has nothing to do with it. The important thing is that she not be a bitch, or arrogant, or a snob, just for starters."

She flashed me an ambiguous smile. She was enjoying herself.

"Shall we say we're also done with insults?" I asked.

She ignored me. "The food here is truly first-class," she said, opening the menu. "Both fish and meat."

I ordered both. A bowl of spaghetti *ai frutti di mare* and a steak an inch thick.

Oriana was irritating even when she ate. The careful accuracy of the movements with which she deboned her gilthead bream in *vernaccia* made me want to pick a fight.

I forced myself to stay focused on the details that could prove useful to me in the investigation. I asked how she communicated with her Guido, what kind of places they went together, bars, restaurants, theaters.

After exactly half an hour of questioning I had to conclude that their affair had been too well-kept a secret for anyone to have been able to find out. It was governed by very precise rules, the same kind that a fugitive or a member of a secret gang might have adopted. She had made very sure that no one would develop even the faintest of suspicions and that, in the unfortunate case that such a thing did happen, there would still be no evidence to bear that suspicion out. All the same, the worst had happened. This illicit, clandestine couple had been spotted and attacked by a gang of criminals.

"Obviously someone must have recognized you," I said. "This morning you told me that several pictures of you have been published in magazines and newspapers."

"Only in the Ticino canton. In Italy I'm completely unknown."

"Did you use a credit card to pay your bills?"

She pierced me with a pitying look. "Cash. All payments exclusively in cash."

"Then the professor must have talked with someone about it," I theorized, having eliminated all other hypotheses. "He must have confided in a friend, or bragged to one: you know what men are like, and that act put in motion the mechanism that led to the kidnapping."

"That's the first thing I thought myself. But Guido isn't the type."

"Wasn't," I corrected her, breaking in. "Put your heart at rest on that point."

"I can't bring myself to do it," she confessed from behind a film of tears that worried me.

"Forgive me, go on, please," I said, doing my best to make up for what I'd said and refilling her glass.

"Yes, he has plenty of friends. He's also a musician, he plays the guitar, but he understood that we'd have to lead double lives if we wanted this relationship to continue. We love each other very much. I am his one true love, his real woman, that much at least is clear to you, isn't it?"

While Signora Pozzi Vitali raved on, dangerously close to the brink of lunacy, I did my best to suppress my despair. I had nothing useful to help me get started on a serious investigation. And by now too much time had gone by. Memories fade, gangs drift apart, criminals move away, and with every day that passes, they erase their tracks with greater and greater care.

I was tempted to tell her so, but it would have been needlessly cruel.

She pulled an envelope out of her bag: it contained the cash and the keys to the apartment in Padua.

"Did Guido have a set of his own?" I asked, for no particular reason.

"No, he wouldn't have known how to explain them away, and Enrica has always been rather inquisitive, you know, one of those women who check trouser pockets and cell phones. Not because they don't trust their men, but rather on principle, because they believe that in a relationship, when the man steps out, he needs to be roped back in immediately."

"But that's not the way you see things, is it?"

"Only a petty bourgeois from the bottom of the barrel could humiliate herself like that," she replied testily. "I've always taken it for granted that Ugo was cheating on me, and after a number of years of marriage it even came as a relief since it freed me from my weekly matrimonial obligations."

She caught a waiter's attention. "Would you be so good as to bring me a crème caramel? And you, Signor Buratti?"

CHAPTER THREE

I walked into the law offices of Counselor Bonotto and handed my cell phone to his secretary. The lawyer was talking to a guy who looked about forty-five and was wearing a spectacularly garish short-sleeved Hawaiian shirt. He looked me up and down, quizzically.

Bonotto stood up, adjusted his jacket, and held out his hand.

"It's been a while, Marco."

"Yeah, a few years I'd say," I shot back. I wasn't in the mood for idle chitchat.

"Let me introduce you to Inspector Campagna," he went on. I turned toward him and shook hands. "Buratti."

"Giulio Campagna, robbery division," he introduced himself.

"Before I leave the two of you alone," Bonotto clarified, "it strikes me that I ought to go over the facts that have brought you here today. Marco, a man I know and respect, asked if I was in contact with a member of law enforcement with whom he could talk about a certain situation, someone whose absolute discretion he could trust.

"I thought immediately of Inspector Campagna, in whom I have implicit faith, and I asked him if he would be willing to hear what Buratti had to say. Based on his assurances of complete confidentiality, I arranged this meeting."

The cop raised his hand. "Of course, the terms apply as long as Buratti is not directly involved in any wrongdoing, otherwise he'll be walking out of this office in handcuffs."

"Of course," I confirmed, trying to get a sense of the man.

At first glance, he struck me as a tough character, rigid and intractable. I hoped he would be turn out to be smart as well.

The lawyer stood up, picked up his briefcase, and left the room.

"I know who you are," the inspector told me straight off. "So let's skip the preliminaries."

I offered him a cigarette. He took it, stood up, turned off the air conditioner, and opened the window. A gust of hot muggy air blew in. Clouds heavy with rain covered the sky. Luckily the sidewalks in downtown Padua were lined with porticoes.

"Two lovers. She is wealthy, he's an academic who lives on his salary," I began, doing my best to be clear and concise. "The woman imposes maniacal security measures, but one fine day she receives a phone call from a stranger telling her to hand over three hundred thousand euros' worth of jewelry in a few days' time, or else the man will die. She severs all ties and the male lover hasn't been heard from since."

"When is this all supposed to have happened?"

"March 14th, 2013."

"Have the police come up with anything?"

I shook my head. "The man is still listed as a missing person."

The detective crushed out his cigarette butt on the windowsill and sat down in the lawyer's office chair. "These plastic chairs cost an arm and a leg and they're uncomfortable too," he said, changing the subject just to give himself time to think.

"Kidnapping for ransom is a crime of the past," he began, thinking out loud. "When they figured out that we always eventually caught them, because kidnapping required too many gang members to keep leaks from springing, they pretty much dropped the whole thing.

"Then there was the period, much shorter, of kidnappings 'on the fly.' They'd demand thirty to a hundred million lire and release the hostage in the space of twenty-four hours. But back then people had an easier time laying their hands on cash.

These days the banks give us a call whenever they get a suspicious request.

"But now, according to what you're telling me, a gang has kidnapped a guy with no money and tried to extort his wealthy lover."

"That's exactly right."

"And all of us at headquarters are entirely in the dark."

"Precisely."

"How lucky that the great unlicensed private detective has turned up and is determined to break the case wide open with my help."

He didn't like me. But I stayed where I was for one reason: I needed him.

"I think we could both help each other out, that is, if you're still interested."

"I'm certainly in no position to just let a kidnapping and a murder go. If what you say turns out to be true, then someone needs to be sent to prison for life without parole, but I want one thing to be clear from the start: to me you're nothing but a confidential informant, and that's how I'm going to treat you. Don't think for a second that you can play at being my 'partner.' That's not going to work with me."

He was going over the top. "I wouldn't dream of it," I retorted drily. "I've never liked cops or informants. The offer on the table involves the two of us working together in an atmosphere of mutual trust, sharing whatever we find. If you don't like that, I'll leave right now and never bother you again."

He gave me a slap on the shoulder. "Sorry, Buratti, I just wanted to make sure I wasn't dealing with some wing nut who thinks he's Nero Wolfe or with some brownnosing informer."

"I thought you'd asked around about me."

"Old news. You've been missing from our fair city for far too long, I'd have been a sucker to rely on what little I was able to find out."

He wasn't exactly a barrel of fun, but maybe the attorney had introduced me to the right cop. I brought him up to speed on the details, leaving out only the truly useless ones. "I don't have the resources to investigate Guido Di Lello in Rome," I said. "His work environment, his friends, his family. Everything points to the idea that he was the one who talked about his affair with Oriana Pozzi Vitali. Here in Padua, so far, my partner and I haven't found even the faintest shred of evidence."

I looked at him. I'd let slip the detail that I worked with another person and Campagna hadn't blinked, which meant that he already knew all about Max. This cop knew what he was doing.

"It's not going to be easy for me either," he said. "Here I can operate no problem, but if I want to investigate down in Rome I'm going to have to ask, and give, favors."

A few minutes later I found myself strolling through city squares and piazzas crowded with stalls and people out shopping. Padua hadn't changed a bit. The new coalition had won the municipal elections with a campaign focused on security and the fight against urban decay, promising to eliminate intrusive panhandlers, Roma camps, prostitution on the streets, illegal immigrants, and all the other irritations of modern European life. The new leaders of the city were, however, canny enough to understand that when they went too far, they had to recalibrate, and in a hurry. An acrobat from southern Italy, particularly beloved by the citizenry, had objected when he was threatened by city cops who didn't want him to perform just a stone's throw from the renowned Caffè Pedrocchi. When he announced that he was ready to set fire to himself in the public square, suddenly the mayor himself discovered that he'd always been a huge fan of street performers.

The politicians were plying their trade, the people of Padua were satisfied with promises of a "clean" city, but the cocaine trade continued to call the shots downtown. The faces of pushers, old and new, local and foreign, alternated with those of informants, cops, former escorts, young boys and girls eager to trade sex for drugs and cash. And then there were the buyers. Lots of them, all discreet. The merry-go-round went on spinning.

I'd been here for a couple of weeks and I was feeling much better. I was focused on the investigation, keeping nightmares and ghosts at bay. The fact that we were in the saddle again as unlicensed private detectives meant Max was finding his footing again too. He'd taken up old habits and now he spent hours archiving information, though not before fully mastering the kitchen in the apartment that Oriana Pozzi Vitali had so kindly put at our disposal.

The kitchen was elegant, beautiful, and equipped with everything a great chef could desire. But nothing had been used even once until we showed up. The couple hadn't eaten anything but snacks and breakfasts here. Clearly the Swiss woman had wanted her relationship to inhabit a full, vital space, rather than the temporary one most love nests occupy.

Every room was furnished as if it were lived in every day. And not just by two people. Three bedrooms, a study, two bathrooms, a living room, and a kitchen on the top floor of an apartment building on Corso Milano. From the window of my room, I could see the roof of the Teatro Verdi and other views of Padua that had certainly been factored into the purchase price.

That house spoke eloquently of the strength of Oriana's love for her professor. The spectacular warmth of the furnishings aside, when you opened armoires, cabinets, and dresser drawers there was no mistaking the care she had taken to make her lover comfortable.

For once I felt sorry for that odious woman now holed up in an exclusive clinic in Lugano, a place that was well known for taking in famous people who had a few screws loose. The illicit affair with Guido had been a discreet attempt to flee an environment that had forced her to deny her own emotions.

But she'd been unlucky. And the professor even more so. If the corpse hadn't been found yet, it must have been buried or otherwise efficiently disposed of.

During all those days wasted in trying to hunt down a lead of some kind, I had done nothing but think about the gang of kidnappers. I'd known criminals at every level, but these had to be special in some way. The idea had been brilliant in its way: to blackmail a wealthy woman who'd be unlikely to go to the police, and to come prepared with a very specific demand—not even a particularly outrageous one, given the woman's personal wealth—for jewelry, not cash. In other words, the gang was well informed about certain essential details. They knew where, how, and when. It had all been nicely planned. The criminals had invested time and resources. They were capable of kidnapping a man in broad daylight without leaving witnesses, no weapons leveled, no tires screeching. And they'd been capable of disappearing into thin air without leaving the slightest trace.

They couldn't have gone to all that trouble just for that one kidnapping. It had to be a gang of specialists who had done this before, and since. Their victims had simply chosen to remain silent. Individuals vulnerable to blackmail. People having affairs.

Max and I had checked out neighbors, local cafés, and shops. My partner had trawled the Internet. The professor's fiancée's despair, which she had made public on her Facebook page, aside, the question remained: why had he vanished? No one had dreamed he could have been a victim of a gang that targeted lovers.

Two weeks of completely fruitless investigations had persuaded me that the only lead that could light a way through the impenetrable fog shrouding the case in mystery had to be in Rome. Only Di Lello could have caused the fatal breach of security, whether intentionally or inadvertently. And it was up to Campagna to find out how and when the professor had begun to dig his own grave.

CHAPTER FOUR

He never should have agreed to meet the Alligator. Giulio Campagna kept repeating this to himself as he pedaled toward police headquarters. For some time now he'd been wondering whether he was up to the stresses of his job. He'd migrated from one department to another, playing the part of a cop who dressed eccentrically, didn't suffer hierarchies gladly, and was constantly at odds with his colleagues because of his stubborn determination to conduct investigations his own way. He'd become a loner, no one wanted to team up with him.

The truth was that the inspector was a troubled man. Working for years in narcotics, he'd witnessed the slow but unstoppable triumph of organized crime, the impossibility of putting a halt to drug dealing and drug use. A lost battle that every damn day of the year demanded some new and greater tribute. Giulio had asked to be transferred to the robbery squad, but even there, things were more or less the same. Armed robberies were less frequent than they once had been because the underworld had shifted its strategies and targets, not because police work had done anything to dismantle the networks behind that type of crime.

Campagna never ceased to be amazed at the speed with which new crimes were dreamed up and tried out. What Buratti's story had revealed was serious and worrisome. He had to put a stop to it at all costs.

He suddenly lurched to a halt. Anxiety had emptied his lungs of air. He pretended to study the window of one of the scores of shoe stores, trying to calm himself. Inside, a bored clerk was leafing through a magazine. Shops like this one seemed to be popping up like mushrooms these days. They were always empty and yet they rang up dozens and dozens of sales. The miracles of economic downturns. But money laundering helped a limping economy and these days everyone turned a blind eye. Even him.

When he'd chosen to become a cop, he could never have imagined that the day would come when he'd have to pick and choose which crimes to prosecute because law enforcement lacked the resources to pursue them all.

"We are the ones keeping a sinking boat afloat, bailing out the bilge with a teaspoon," an old cop had told him, just before quitting the force and taking a job as the head of security at a superstore. The man was right, but neither surrendering nor fleeing made any sense. The real problem was trying to figure out whether he was even capable of working for the police anymore.

Campagna was sure that he was, even if he suspected that depression by this point was nipping at his heels. He'd never wanted to dig too deeply, lest he be forced to admit it. He was so widely disliked that they were likely to take advantage of the fact to relegate him to a desk covered with dead case files until he reached retirement age. His tantrums and his solitary investigations helped him to keep that profound and obscure sense of discomfort under control. Even at home, with his family. He finally managed to get his breathing back under control once he managed to admit to himself that this new investigation that the Alligator had served him on a silver tray would help him to keep his head above water. He was well aware, however, that it would be no walk in the park.

Marco Buratti, aka the Alligator, had a reputation as a crusader, one of those guys obsessed with the truth. Once he sank his teeth into a case, he wouldn't let up until he'd solved it. But there were three problems. The first was that Buratti was operating outside the law, since he wasn't authorized to pursue investigations; the second was that he was notorious for getting himself and everyone around him into trouble; and finally there was the fact that he worked with two questionable characters. Max the Memory had a history as an extreme left-wing militant and had been forced to go into hiding. He had also spent a certain period of time in prison. The other one, Beniamino Rossini, had a criminal record a mile long and a reputation for wearing a number of bracelets on his wrist that matched the number of men he'd shot to death.

To sweep away all and any doubts, he thought about that innocent man, kidnapped and murdered. He deserved justice and respect. And his full attention.

An hour later, the inspector handed the file on the disappearance of Professor Guido Di Lello back to his colleague. It contained nothing useful and ventured no theories. People disappear every day, sometimes never to be seen again. Amen.

Campagna was perplexed. He didn't know exactly what to do next and, as he always did when faced with these kinds of situations, he went to knock on the door of the chief of the Mobile Squad, knowing he was about to ruin the man's day.

Calandra welcomed him with a look of obvious irritation, staring at the pattern of white-and-blue flowers on his shirt. "To what do I owe this unscheduled visit?" he asked dryly. "I don't recall asking to see you. Are you in trouble? Look, I moved heaven and earth to get you assigned to the robbery squad. No one wanted you after the mess you made in narcotics."

The inspector raised both hands theatrically to interrupt.

"Nothing like that. I've just come to ask you a favor."

"As long as it doesn't involve vacation days, promotions, overtime, or reimbursements for expenses," his superior stated flatly.

"I need a contact at the Mobile Squad in Rome. I'm looking for some information."

"Follow standard procedures and talk to your chief. That's his responsibility."

"The thing is, this isn't a robbery case."

The chief grew suspicious. "Are you working a case without authorization?"

"No. But I want to."

"What's the story?"

"I've confirmed through a reliable source that a person whom we believe to be missing since March 2013 was actually kidnapped for ransom and then murdered when the ransom wasn't paid."

The chief pointed his forefinger toward the floor. "And here in Padua we knew nothing about it?"

"It seems certain that the man was kidnapped here in the city."

"And just who would this reliable source be?"

"It's better if you never know," the inspector said carefully. "But what I do want to make clear is that if we ever do manage to discover the truth, it won't necessarily be possible to make the facts public."

"Giulio, would you explain to me once and for all why the fuck you always seem to get tangled up in these complicated messes?" his boss exclaimed. "You're telling me that you want to use police department resources to pursue investigations that might never make it into a court of law?"

"That's a risk."

The squad chief grabbed a box of breath mints. He tossed a couple into his mouth and chewed on them with irritation. Campagna knew him well, otherwise he'd never have dared come to him with a request that was so clearly out of bounds. As he had had plenty of opportunities to learn in the past, his boss wasn't the kind of cop who let his men fabricate evidence to toss someone into jail, even when everyone knew they were guilty of something, which was the kind of thing that Giulio had done without a twinge of remorse. But he was a cop through and through, and if, on the other hand, the objective was to keep a crime from going unpunished, he was willing to bend the rules and sidestep procedures. And forget to inform the district attorney's office, while he was at it.

Calandra grabbed the receiver and asked to be put through to his colleague in the capital. After a friendly exchange of small talk, he forged ahead with an explanation of the reason for the phone call, though he limited himself to a brief description of the professor's disappearance. "If you have no objections, I'll send an inspector from my office down tomorrow—someone in whom I place the utmost trust—so that he can clarify certain key elements . . ."

The chief of the Mobile Squad sighed after hanging up. "You'll need to ask for Inspector Valerio Robutti. He's as much of a pain in the ass as you are and, just like you, he's bound and determined to sabotage his career. The two of you will get along famously."

"What am I supposed to say to the section chief?"

"I'll talk to Buccheri myself. Now get going, and come back to see me if and only if we can start an investigative file; otherwise don't bother me because I don't want to hear about it."

The inspector stopped at the front desk to chat with the officers on duty, waiting for the downpour to let up. Before heading home astride his beat-up old bicycle, a family heirloom with old-fashioned rod brakes, he wanted to drop by his favorite wine bar for a glass of white wine. He was one of the very few denizens of the Veneto region under the age of seventy who didn't drink spritzes. He loved aromatic white wines, those from Friuli and Trentino, and just then he needed their company. A glass of wine, a cigarette, and a chance to shoot the breeze. These things served as a kind of detox, wiping work from his mind before he headed home. In the past, his inability to let go of his work had come close to costing him his wife and daughter. It had taken a tremendous effort to keep his family together and he'd never again forgotten the lesson.

The rain showed no respect for his thirst and Giulio decided to leave his beloved bicycle in the garage at headquarters and accept a ride offered by a colleague.

He found the two women in his life intently running down the online checklist of textbooks. School was starting in just ten days and already parents and students were restless with anticipation.

"You won't believe the money we're going to have to spend this year," his wife complained. "It's a good thing we bring home two paychecks, I can't imagine how other people manage to lay out this kind of money with the way the economy's going."

Campagna nodded, remembering for the umpteenth time that she made more money than he did. She was a first-rate architect and, unlike lots of other people in her profession, she'd never wanted for work.

He pulled open the fridge and uncorked a bottle of pinot grigio. Gaia joined him and pulled two wineglasses out of the dish rack. "What a shitty summer," he complained, staring out the window. "It's never once stopped raining."

"And what an unforgettable vacation," she said, adding her own two cents. "Three days of sunshine in two weeks."

"We'll make up for it with Christmas in the mountains," Ilaria broke in loudly from the living room. "I can't wait to go skiing."

Campagna looked over at his wife and rubbed his thumb against his index finger in the universal symbol for cash; he wanted to go skiing as much as his daughter did, but it all depended on money.

She sighed. "Plus I need a new car. The mechanic said the one I'm driving now isn't long for this world."

Campagna's wine went down his windpipe. "You should get a second opinion," he choked out while coughing. "Maybe we just need a more optimistic mechanic."

Gaia burst out laughing and started setting the table.

"What's for dinner?" the inspector asked. The wine was starting to stir his appetite.

"Stuffed peppers, stuffed tomatoes, and stuffed calamari."

"You went to see your mother today," he concluded unenthusiastically.

"I've always known you were an exceptional detective," his wife ribbed him, putting on the voice of who-knows-which television character.

"I have to go to Rome tomorrow," Campagna announced, clarifying immediately that he'd be traveling for work. "I'll be gone a couple of days, at most."

Gaia wrapped her arms around him. "Then you'd better get busy tonight, or when you miss me you'll start to get strange thoughts . . ."

With a hint of panic, Giulio Campagna sensed that this wasn't the night for it. Too much on his mind. He went into the bathroom and swallowed a tablet that the doctor at the reproductive health clinic had prescribed.

"Better living through chemistry," he muttered, heaving a sigh of relief.

Robutti was a big, bearded man with a strong Ligurian accent. He greeted the colleague from Padua with unmistakable mistrust. "What's behind this trip?" he asked, cutting straight to the chase.

Campagna looked him square in the eye to gauge how far he could risk going.

The other man clearly had no time to waste. He slammed one hand down hard on his desk. "My boss calls me up and tells me to hurry up and scrape together all the information I can find about a case nobody gives a good goddamn about and to put myself completely at your service. Which I'm delighted to do, of course, but I want to know what this is all about, I'm not going to blunder into something I'm in the dark about."

The man had a point. "Kidnapping and murder," Giulio put it tersely. "We're working to identify those responsible, but discreetly."

"How discreetly?"

"As discreetly as necessary."

"Which means nobody knows a fucking thing," Robutti laughed with gusto as he handed over the file. With that gesture, the inspector made clear he was willing to help and didn't need to be looped in on other details. Campagna thanked him with a smile.

He started leafing through the various police reports. Nothing useful, just routine checks and rundowns. "I was hoping to find something I didn't already know," said the policeman from Padua as he carefully studied the first decent photograph he'd seen of Guido Di Lello.

A pointy little face, made manly and just barely interesting by a mustache and goatee, glasses with very light frames, dark eyes that protruded slightly, a shifty gaze, longish wavy hair hanging over his collar. He felt a twinge of disappointment and wondered just what his wealthy lover had found so irresistible.

"This poor idiot was a complete dick face, I have to say," Robutti commented, without malice. "Still, I've done a fair bit of work for you and I've more than earned the lunch that you're going to treat me to in less than an hour," he announced, pulling a steno pad fat with scribbled notes out of his desk drawer.

It took him a few minutes to summarize dates, identities, family ties, and street addresses, before revealing his true skills as a first-rate investigator. "Having no idea as to the reasons for your request but guessing that they were fairly serious, I did my best to flesh out the individual's personality," he clarified as he glanced through his notes. "This Guido Di Lello wasn't especially well liked in academic circles. He was one of those guys who thinks the world is against him. He'd write articles viciously

closed-circuit surveillance cameras and citizens who were all too willing to testify in court. But the professor had stepped off the train and vanished into thin air. And now it was his job to get back on that same train and go home in search of a clue, any clue at all.

"I hope you're taking me somewhere that serves good Roman cuisine. *Pasta all'amatriciana, spaghetti alla carbonara . . .*" Giulio said, changing the subject.

"Not on your life! I'm from Savona. A fellow Ligurian has started a trattoria here that makes me think I'm back at my mother's table."

Giulio couldn't manage to restrain a grimace of disappointment. Robutti shook his head and snickered. "All right, all right, I'll take you out for a *rigatoni alla pajata* that's out of this world. But you don't know what you're missing . . . for that matter, you're from the Veneto and you all are certainly anything but gourmands, all you have is a couple of pathetic ragtag recipes."

"Don't push it," Campagna said, mock-menacingly. "Otherwise I'll keep certain pieces of gossip to myself that, I assure you, are juicier than the *capòn magro.*"

CHAPTER FIVE

I wondered why Campagna had decided to dress like a country bumpkin. It wasn't just that he had terrible taste in clothes; it was clearly a conscious choice. There was a time in my life when I dressed like a blues singer from Louisiana but the reason was that I was trying to stand out, trying to tell the world I had once been a musician, after jail had thoroughly ruined my singing voice. Now I missed my python skin boots, the belts with buckles that weighed in at close to two pounds of scrap metal, the stovepipe jeans, and the garishly colored raw linen shirts, but at a certain point the basic imperatives of survival had forced me to start dressing like everyone else. That change hadn't been painless. I'd started shopping in clothing stores where the clerks did their best once they understood I was a hopeless case, and I just let them try.

But Campagna did everything imaginable to stick out like a sore thumb, even though you'd expect a plainclothes cop to do the opposite. The new generation of European criminals had become more discreet, sartorially speaking, and the inspector violated the boundaries of good taste both for an on-duty cop and for a criminal. Like every eccentric, he proudly made his home in no-man's-land.

That's what I was thinking about while I waited for him in the parking lot of a buffet-style restaurant in an industrial park. Max wasn't talking. I'd practically had to arm-wrestle him into coming to meet him, and the last thing he wanted to do was be introduced to a cop.

"Campagna knows that you exist and that you and I are both working on this case," I'd said, exasperated, after his thousandth objection. "And after all, it's better for there to be the two of us listening to what he has to say."

The inspector had phoned ahead from the train on his way back from Rome. He needed to meet with me, urgently. I was hoping he was bringing good news until the instant I saw him step out of his car. The twist in his lips spoke clearly of weariness born of a long trip made in vain.

Max and the cop shook hands without introducing themselves.

"These days, it takes just over three hours to reach Rome by train," the policeman began, as if chatting with someone at the bar. "That means you can get up at six and by midmorning you're already in the offices of the Mobile Squad, where an amiable fellow cop can sweep away any hopes you might have of figuring out anything about this fucked-up case. And rightly so. The Roman trail is useless. Even if the whole thing had its origins in the academic world, there's no way we can track it down."

Campagna pressed a hand to his stomach. "I can't seem to digest the *rigatoni alla pajata* that I ate."

"That happens when you forget to include cloves," Max explained in the tone of voice of a know-it-all. "At least one clove for every pound of intestine. Veal tripe, of course. I wouldn't recommend beef tripe."

The inspector shot him a look too admiring to be real. "You sure know about cooking. That's not mentioned in your file. A passion you developed recently to help you get over some larger political defeat?"

The fat man sat openmouthed, aghast at the detective's shameless presumption.

"Don't take the bait," I warned him. "The inspector is a bit of a prankster, he's just pushing your buttons."

Campagna put on a tense smile and went on talking about the case. "What doesn't make sense to me is that there were no witnesses to the kidnapping. And yet it was broad daylight and there were plenty of cameras along the route, to say nothing of all the passersby."

"Maybe he just showed up at an appointment he should have skipped," the fat man put in.

"Maybe," echoed the detective. "The only investigative lead I'm inclined to suggest is to check out the most recently formed gangs. I won't be able to dedicate myself to it full-time since my boss just told me that I need to focus on a team of Italian-Albanian armed robbers, so don't expect results anytime soon."

"All right," I said. "Let's hope we have better luck."

"What's your plan?" asked the inspector.

"We still don't really have one," I told him honestly.

"After all, your Swiss matron will be paying for whatever you do," he quipped acidly. "And I'd love to know just how much."

"Let's get out of here, Marco," said the fat man, clearly offended, heading for the car that we'd picked up at the dealership just a few hours earlier. "We're just wasting our time."

I held out a hand to Campagna, who clasped it firmly. "You just can't get over the idea that, since you're a cop, you're a cut above us," I said in a weary tone of voice.

He shook his head. "You're wrong, Buratti; I just can't stand the idea that you guys are pocketing more money than I take home, and all completely off the books, because you don't have so much as the hint of a license in your pockets."

I turned on my heels and went over to my partner.

"And you made me travel all this way so I could listen to that lunatic cop insult me?" Max said, indignantly.

I waved to him to shut up. "I want to enjoy the ritual of turning over the engine, I want to fill my ears with the roar of a Škoda engine," I said, improvising freely just to cut the tension.

"And your mental health is even worse than his," the fat man hissed ferociously. "We drove all over the Veneto region like a couple of idiots in search of this jalopy."

"What jalopy?" I objected. "This is a 2001 Felicia, from the last year of production."

"Even the dealer didn't want to sell it to you."

"Because he wanted to sell me a brand-new model."

"Do you know that we're the only people even driving a Felicia? There aren't any more on the roads these days. Everyone's gotten rid of them."

"That's not true. I'm pretty sure that my friend the guitarist Paolo Valentini is at the wheel of his pride and joy right now."

"Just like this one? Green with an orange trunk lid?"

I snorted. "As soon as I have a spare minute I'll take it in to the body shop to have it repainted. Don't harp on it. It's a car that no one notices, no one gives it a second glance."

"Fine. But have you noticed that this September is a hot one and a little humid too from time to time, and your Felicia didn't come equipped with air conditioning?"

"If I buy you dinner, will you stop making me pay for the bad mood Campagna put you in?"

He turned suddenly to look at me. "Is it that obvious?"

I nodded. "You need to bury it under just the right amount of food and wine, Max. Choose a restaurant from the list our client provided."

With a certain effort he pulled a rumpled notebook out of his back pocket. "Signora Oriana Pozzi Vitali and Professor Di Lello enjoyed a table at seven restaurants in the surrounding area. They even went to a few of them more than once."

The fat man tossed the notebook against the inside of the windshield. "Fine, I may just be in a bad mood, but this idea of a pilgrimage to the various restaurants seems ridiculous."

"If we start applying this approach to our investigation we can just give up right now."

"Who do you think might have noticed them?" the fat man

insisted. "And even if they did, so what? You think some guy saw them eating and talking and just decided to put a gang together and kidnap Di Lello?"

"You're probably right, Max," I admitted, doing my best to make him think. "But we have nothing to go on and just a short while ago Campagna showed up empty-handed. Experience has taught us that you should never overlook anything."

He lit two cigarettes and handed me one. "Fine. Just don't make me talk to that cop again."

"He's less of an asshole than you think he is. He just hasn't managed to keep up with the times and he feels out of place."

"Spare me that nonsense, Marco. And head for the highway. We're going to Vicenza to have some *baccalà*."

"Isn't it a little too hot for salted cod?"

"No," he replied tersely. "And don't embarrass me with these awkward questions while we order. Leave it to me and everything will go smoothly."

Tuesday, Wednesday, and Thursday. Three days, three restaurants. No complaints in terms of the quality of the food or the waitstaff, but they were completely wasted expeditions as far as the investigation was concerned. We doled out princely tips to waiters and valet parking attendants only to be told that no one remembered the professor, even though his picture had been published in plenty of newspapers and broadcast on TV. No one had ever noticed any questionable characters, save the usual coke dealers and high-end whores, but by now those were just part of the scenery. One restaurant was equipped with closed-circuit TV cameras but the tapes were erased every week. Just to satisfy our curiosity, we paid to view the last three days. Hours and hours of boredom.

Friday night we went to La Nena. Reservations were required for dinner but luckily a couple had cancelled just a few minutes before we walked in. As they started us off with an excellent prosecco, Max and I exchanged a glance and a grin. That place really was patronized by the crème de la crème: outsourced industrialists and the professionals who serviced them with the adroit agility of tightrope walkers, low-end politicians with "bribe me" stamped on their foreheads, shopkeepers whose businesses were kept afloat by a little loan sharking on the side accompanied by sales clerks decked out like paid escorts. A portrait of Veneto—deeply ingrained and impossible to uproot—as greedy, vulgar, and parasitic.

The owner of the place was drop-dead handsome with an irresistible smile that everyone swooned over. He moved from table to table as if he were a movie star.

He stopped by ours too. "Everything all right?" he asked, eyeing us with an entomologist's clinical scrutiny. "I'm the owner and you can call me Giorgio."

"A pleasure," said Max. "We're just taking a look at the menu."

"Take all the time you need. And if you need any advice don't hesitate to call me," he said, before moving on to the next table.

The whole place was impeccable. Every detail was born of a very specific idea of how to run a restaurant. The guest should feel perfectly at ease while enjoying a regional cuisine reinterpreted by a young chef, fresh off a round of awards and television appearances.

The clients were regulars, for the most part. They all seemed to know each other, launching jokes from one table to another. The rest were tourists or people drawn by the excellent reviews in specialty magazines.

"The food is very good here," the fat man decreed as he wiped his mouth with an ivory cloth napkin. "And it doesn't strike me as the kind of place where you'd run into the criminals we're looking for."

I took one last look at the diners. "Many of them are knee-deep in business and finance. You can't rule out the possibility that someone recognized Signora Pozzi Vitali."

Max mimed clutching at straws. "One thing we can rule out with 100 percent confidence, though," he said, gesturing around the dining room. "No one recognized the professor."

We burst out laughing and just then the proprietor came over, accompanied by two ladies. "Laughter is always the best medicine," he said; his tone was ambiguous enough that I found it vaguely offensive. "Would you mind if these two lovely maidens joined your table? Otherwise I'll be obliged to show them the door, and I'd be especially sorry to do so, since one of them is my wife," he said, pointing to a woman who hastened to introduce herself as Martina.

"And I'm Gemma," put in the other one. "The girlfriend."

We helped them get seated, a little awkwardly because we would have preferred to be left alone.

The proprietor's spouse was a recapitulation of the restaurant itself in human form. Perfect, impeccable, charming, but not excessively so. Everything about her was measured. The other one was different, much more similar to the other women eating in the restaurant. She downed Martina's bubbly without asking permission, as if by habit. And she gulped her antipasto in just a couple of bites. Max and I were far too familiar with life's disasters not to notice the boundless sea of unhappiness in which this woman was drowning. Of the two, there was no mistaking the fact that Gemma was more perceptive and smarter. Martina seemed somehow lobotomized.

After the usual chitchat and remarks on how odd the weather had been that summer, a long silence descended. The two women, perhaps feeling guilty about having invaded our table, began sounding out our willingness to converse with them. When they told us that they often wound up sitting with strangers, given the fact that they ate at La Nena every night, the two of us suddenly turned talkative, and in just a few minutes both women were attentively studying Professor Di Lello's face.

Martina summoned her husband over with a wave of the hand. "Giorgio, honey, have you ever seen this gentleman?" she asked, handing him the photo.

"No, I'm afraid I haven't," he said calmly and then fired off a sharp, specific question. "Are you two gentlemen from the police force?"

"No," I replied.

"Then I can't understand why you would come to my restaurant and start showing that photograph around." His tone of voice was not threatening, much less discourteous.

"Pure curiosity," the fat man retorted brusquely.

Giorgio placed both hands on the shoulders of his wife and her friend. "Watch out for these two busybodies," he joked before returning to his duties as a restaurateur.

Suddenly Martina decided to torture us by changing the subject to outlet stores. Not just one in particular, but all the outlets within a two hundred kilometer radius. By dessert I was ready to beg for mercy. Max, equally tested by the grueling ordeal, didn't ask for a second round of grappa.

"Did everything meet with your satisfaction?" the proprietor asked at the cash register.

"Yes, thanks."

"Then I'll look forward to seeing you again. Come back whenever you like."

In order to recover from our close encounter with that lunatic of a wife of his, we stopped to drink a beer. The evening was hot, the piazza was dotted with little café tables.

"Strange pair of girlfriends," I noted.

"What the hell got into her? There was no way to get her to shut up or change the subject. And I didn't like her husband one bit. Did you see how he reacted when we showed the professor's photo? It was as if we were polluting his restaurant."

"Maybe we made a mistake by not pushing the staff a little harder."

"It would have just been a waste of time. Three more days and we'll be done with our culinary tour. Not that I've minded, the Lord only knows, but I think it's clear that our two illicit lovers didn't get themselves into trouble between the risotto and the chicken cacciatore," Max concluded.

CHAPTER SIX

I'd sniffed them out the second they set foot in La Nena. Then, when they'd pulled out the picture of that asshole, I'd had my proof. They weren't cops, nor did they come out of the private sector. They were mercenaries. What I didn't understand was how they'd managed to track me down. I immediately put in a call to Federico Togno, former carabiniere, former private detective, former perennially unlucky patron of the gambling dens of Northeastern Italy, former coke hound. He'd ruined his life for no particular reason because it wasn't worth a damn to him. His role in the world was to serve. I'd picked him up out of poverty and set him back on his feet a couple of years ago, and ever since he'd tagged along after me like a loyal lapdog. I'd secured him a house and even a wife, Maria José Pagliaro, a prostitute just as short on brains as he was; she was a pain in the ass left over from when I was forced to close up shop as a pimp. She'd decided, and not without good reason, that all her former colleagues had come to ugly ends, and she'd said that she was willing to do anything I asked if I'd spare her life.

I'd told her the truth. "Believe me, they're all fine, it's just that I sent them to work somewhere far away."

"I don't want to go far away," Maria José had whispered.

Even if she wasn't at all bad looking, I didn't know what to do with her. I'd screwed her a few times without enjoying it even a little. The only thing she was good for was as a wife, so I'd married her off to Federico.

"It's your job to make my little soldier happy," I had instructed her. "Make sure his cock is slick and shiny and keep an eye on him for me. Once a month you'll come give me a full report."

So I'd been able to rely on Federico with a certain margin of safety. I used him as a driver, bodyguard, and investigator for 3,000 euros a month. In the past, when I wanted information, I'd made use of other lowlifes with police ties, but he was just rotten enough and might bring me better results. Little by little I'd gotten him used to the idea that there were times when violence was necessary. A couple of broken bones, a break-in or two, a rape. When Maria José let me know that her husband had enjoyed those experiences, I assigned him his first killing. A nice, easy job. A Maghrebi immigrant who had decided to bother my customers by grabbing purses right outside the restaurant. The fifth or sixth time it happened, I made up my mind that taking him out was the only way to rid the city of that parasite. Federico was up to the challenge. A portico, a winter's night. Ali Baba was laying his last ambush when he was stabbed; the blade sliced through his right kidney.

After, I demonstrated my generosity, sending my hired killer and his wife on a ten-day vacation at a resort in Tunisia. That locale hadn't been chosen at random, but he'd failed to detect the irony in the concealed reference to the victim's place of origin.

That night I'd ordered him to tail those two assholes and now I was waiting for him to come back and feeling a bit anxious. It was getting late and I was in a hurry to find out as many details as possible so that I could react appropriately.

If I had been found out, others would soon be showing up, and certainly not to pay the kind of astronomical check I'd saddled those two with. That said, the looks on their faces when I'd gone over to their table had hardly indicated suspicion.

Some tiny nugget of evidence must have led them to La Nena, but the situation could still be considered well under control.

My henchman knocked at the restaurant door at 2:30 A.M. "Sorry, Giorgio, but first those guys had a couple of beers out here in the piazza, then it took them forever to get to Padua. You know they get around in a Škoda that's old as the hills?"

"Once they got to Padua, where did they go?"

"They parked on Corso Milano. Then I saw them walk into an apartment building, at number 78."

I was struck by the fact that they were living in the secret hideout of the two pathetic lovebirds. They seemed like natives of the Veneto, not outsiders: the fat man talked like a typical Paduan.

"I have to find out who they are, Federico. And fast."

"I have their license number and a couple of pictures I snapped with my cell phone. I can ask Brigadier Stanzani for a favor; he's on duty in Padua. He's a dear friend of mine but he certainly doesn't stick his neck out for nothing."

"How much does he want?"

From his smirk I understood it wouldn't be money. "A woman, cocaine . . . We're set up to make him happy."

"A complete evening out. Dinner and then a whore in a luxury hotel."

I thought how cute it would be to send Maria José. She had the necessary experience to make him enjoy all the delights of corruption. I resisted the urge. "You'll take care of everything, right?"

Federico nodded. "Tomorrow afternoon at the latest I'll let you have the first batch of information."

I turned off the lights, activated the alarm, and finally went home. Martina and Gemma were dozing on the sofa in front of the TV, waiting to receive their instructions for the night. Usually I issued directives at dinner in the restaurant, but those two snoops had distracted me.

"Good night, Martina," I said and she stood up, docile as always, gave me a kiss, and headed for the bedroom.

Gemma came to me and started unlacing my shoes. She'd been living with us for three years now; she'd always been my wife's best friend and I needed someone to keep Martina company. So, when it became clear to me that her husband running off with another woman to Salento had pushed her to the very edge, I started manipulating her. It was what she wanted. She put out very specific signals to that end. She was clearly letting herself go, at times with a kind of abandon. She wasn't a bit stupid and she'd read my intentions. She hated and loved me with the same intensity. She couldn't live without me or the life I offered her because I hadn't left her anything else. Martina never batted an eye, not even when I demanded that she have sex with Gemma. Neither one of them liked it, but for my wife it might as well have been an hour of spinning. For that matter, I was her love forever, the doting husband who made her happy. I deserved complete satisfaction even when I made the most unusual requests.

"Tell me all about those two," I ordered.

"There's not a lot to tell. They showed us that picture, then your wife slayed them with her topic of the month: discount shopping."

"How did they explain that strange request?"

"A friend of theirs who comes often to a restaurant in the center of town sang its praises and they just wanted to make sure that he'd been talking about La Nena."

"What a bullshit excuse," I thought to myself.

"Actually, though, I think I've seen him before."

"Who?"

"That guy in the picture."

"Where?"

"On TV. You know that show about missing people?"

Gemma never missed a chance to rev her brain and let me know about it. It was her way of letting me know she was well aware that I was a criminal.

book, *Il mio Nordest*, had been tossed into the region's recycling bins. Everyone kept his distance. Even the newspaper that had shamelessly brownnosed him back in his glory days now treated him as if he were the most miserable outcast.

His wife and daughters watched from the sidelines as he was forced to submit to the humiliation of a plea bargain: a little over two years in prison and a little over two million euros to be paid back to the Italian state.

It was a way to prevent a dangerous trial during which a delicate equilibrium would have been held in place by the slenderest of wires. The powerful families and their new allies, elected by the people of the Veneto, had achieved their goal of issuing a stark warning to the intricate world of business and politics: the age of Brianese was over, once and for all. No one could ever again claim the right to plunder without sharing.

I had long believed that politics was the pinnacle of criminal creativity. I'd been forced to reconsider. No one, in the end, had been able to achieve liftoff, creating a lasting, stable alliance between the state, systematic corruption, and organized crime. Sante Brianese was the model case study. A corrupt politician is useful only as long as he faithfully does as he's told, otherwise he's just fucking himself over.

The true boundaries are the rules of the game. You can't dedicate yourself to the fine art of theft, extortion, bribery, and money laundering unless you're willing to resort to violence. I'd done my best to explain this to him when we were still on speaking terms, but the Honorable MP and his lover had just gotten scared. To death. Maybe that's why the idea of cutting me in on their deal had never even occurred to them.

As had so often been the case in my life, I'd been once again forced to reinvent myself, professionally speaking. I'd always opted for the kind of criminal pursuit that guaranteed profitability and at the same time helped me achieve personal satisfaction. I'm a predator. I like to possess other people, take over their lives. Control them, exercise mastery over them, and as such wield the power to make them even worse than they already are, keep them from being able to look at themselves in the mirror without a shudder of disgust.

I'd emerged from my clash with Brianese and his Calabrians stronger and richer, and I could have been happy with what I already had. But I never would have been able to put up with the boredom of such a narrow existence, nor would I have been satisfied repeating familiar experiences—turning, for example, to drugs, whores, and robberies. Not only because I needed the thrill of the new, but also because one of the requirements of this line of work is the kind of flexibility that allows you to elude the notice and sanctions of the law. Long-term criminal specialization inevitably leads to a prison cell.

The fact is that not everyone has the capacity and the courage to change. I've always been something of a thoroughbred. A winner. A pioneer. The proof is in the sheer number of crimes I've committed and for which I'll never pay the price. I've never been presented with the check at the end of the meal; if anything I present the check to others at La Nena, my undisputed domain, the treasure that not even the Calabrian *'ndrangheta* has been able to rob me of.

My customers arrive, take their seats, think only of enjoying themselves, blithely unaware that all the while I'm observing them, cataloguing them. I judge whether and to what degree they can be useful to me. One day, at lunch, a guy came in with his fourteen-year-old daughter. He'd made a point of saying that's who she was when he made his reservation. Only I knew that it was a lie. He probably didn't remember, but we'd met a couple of years earlier in Friuli, at some enological-slash-gastronomical initiative for local restaurateurs. His name was Pierluigi Zettina, and he ran a family-owned business that produced first-class prosciutto and salami. His daughter was quite pretty, likable and competent too—only she was twenty-five and the youngest of three siblings. The businessman was fifty-five and he'd made plenty of money; he drove a big, flashy car, but he was ignoring the golden rule that says if you want to fuck a minor without running too many risks, you'd better not take her out in public.

The age difference was unmistakable and unless a physical resemblance instantly certifies paternity, as a rule people are liable to think the worst. I'd watched the two of them carefully, and the man was on pins and needles, swiveling his head constantly, on the lookout for glares of reprobation. This outing must have been the little girl's idea. Maybe she'd thrown a tantrum to get what she wanted and demanded an expensive restaurant to boot. Or else she was just an underage whore on the first rungs of the professional ladder and her pimp wanted to show her off.

Their heads were close as they talked quietly. At a certain point, I noticed her hand fleetingly caress his. Zettina had instantly yanked his hand away, scorching her with an angry glare. It didn't look as if the young babe was a product of the lower middle class. She had a sharp haircut, her jeans and sweater were brand-name. And she was clearly at her ease in a fine restaurant. Before too long I'd figured out she was the one running the show, and that to a certain extent the man obeyed her.

There's a joke I've always liked about a guy who finds himself tied to a tree. A car pulls over to help him, and he tells the driver about the insane day he's having, how fate has unleashed its fury on him, plaguing him with mishap after mishap. The last piece of bad luck involved an attack by an armed robber who not only took his car and all his belongings, but left him bound to the tree with a rope. The good Samaritan listens in silence, then with a smile tells him how sorry he is, drops his trousers, and ass-rapes him.

When presented with the perverse fragility of that man's situation I felt the exact same desire to toy with him, to burst into his life with my elbows out. To fuck him over. I suddenly felt relaxed, my mind was agile and alert, there was a pleasant warmth in my gut.

I personally tailed them to a motel halfway between Padua and Venice. Zettina got out of the car to pick up the room key. When thirty minutes had passed, I walked into the front office.

The desk clerk welcomed me with a smile. "Do you have a reservation?"

"No. I need to make a phone call. I'd like to call Room 29."

The man caught a whiff of trouble in the air and was immediately on the defensive. "I don't know if I can allow that. Our guest left no instructions about calls to the room."

"The gentleman in question is entertaining my niece, who is underage, in that room," I explained frostily. "I can always just call the police."

The desk clerk grabbed a pack of cigarettes and a lighter. "I think I'll go have a smoke," he announced.

The businessman picked up on the sixth ring.

"Yes?"

"*Ciao*, Pierluigi."

"Who is this?"

"It's Giorgio, your best friend."

"Who are you? I don't know any Giorgio."

"Tell the girl to get dressed," I said brusquely, cutting him off. "I'm taking her home."

Zettina was immediately plunged into a panic. I had a hard time calming him down. "No one will ever know a thing because we're going to work together to find a way to muzzle my conscience, which tells me to shout from the rooftops that you're a goddamned child molester."

"You don't scare me," the man stammered.

"Not even a little bit, right?" I retorted mockingly. "You're such a tough guy. You'll hold your head up, right through the media firestorm, the trial, the reactions of your family, of *her* family . . ."

The girl came out of the room a few minutes later. She shot me a hate-filled glare through the windshield. I pushed open the passenger-side door. "Get in," I ordered.

She obeyed. She wasn't scared. "It's not what you think," she said. "We're in love."

I burst out laughing. "My name's Giorgio, what's yours?"

"Virginia."

I laughed even harder.

"How old are you?"

"Fourteen."

"Where do you live?"

"In Udine."

I pointed to my GPS navigator. "Type in your address."

"Why are you doing this?" she asked after a while.

"Because at your age you shouldn't go to bed with men forty years older than you."

"We don't have intercourse."

"Oh, really? So what does your handsome Pierluigi do? Does he touch your pussy, lick it? And do you suck his dick?"

The girl's eyes welled over with tears. "Don't talk like that, you make it all sound so dirty."

I shook my head. This poor idiot was actually in love.

"What are you going to do now? Are you going to report him to the police?" she asked between sobs. "He says that he's ready to kill himself."

I gripped her arm and spoke gently. "There's no need for things to go that far. If he shows a little common sense, I won't say a thing to a soul, but I'm going to need you to promise that you won't see him again until you turn sixteen."

"That's impossible. I'm his niece. Our families see each other all the time."

I sighed. "I meant alone, Virginia. No more outings, no more intimate meals in restaurants, no more motels, got it? You're just lucky I'm the one who found you, someone else could have permanently destroyed your reputations. Do you have any idea of the risks that Pierluigi is running? If you really do love him, two years isn't really such a long time."

With that priestly little sermon, I managed to win her trust. She told me everything. Zettina had been wooing her since before she turned twelve.

"You're an idiot," I insulted him as soon as I was face to face with him a couple of hours later. "How long did you think your romance with that little girl was going to last? You're a hop, a skip, and a jump from the border, you can find some girl from a poor family in a shitty village and screw her to your heart's content, with her parents' blessing to boot, like all the other sickos do."

"You don't understand . . ."

I lifted my fist, ready to deck him. "Don't even think of trying to palm the star-crossed lovers shtick off on me. Virginia already busted my balls with that bullshit."

"How much do you want?" he asked in a weary tone of voice. "I have to warn you that I can only pay once, and not very much."

I slapped him jovially on the back. "Don't fret, Pierluigi, I'll be happy to settle for a single truckload, packed to the rafters. Your driver can stop for an espresso along the road and someone with a copy of the keys will make the truck disappear. The insurance company will take care of your losses. As you can see, you're getting off cheap."

"All right," he said.

I waited for him to start walking away. "Of course, you're also going to be holding a tasting party every three months in my restaurant, which starting today you'll be supplying gratis."

"Don't overdo it," he implored. "My children aren't idiots, after all."

I feigned astonishment. "I'm just trying to help you out, Pierluigi, and take my advice: if you want young girls, look east."

Zettina was the first and also the easiest. But he was the least satisfying, too. I'd behaved like a bully who steals the other kids' lunches. I'd reaped a considerable profit, but I hadn't managed to submerge him in that despair made up of shame, fear, and humiliation, the kind of despair that never really goes away. The kind that burrows deep in your heart and can't be uprooted. Pierluigi would learn his lesson, become cannier. But I should have used Virginia, ruined her for good, drowned her in a sea of nightmares. The problem was that I don't like little girls. I like women in their forties. I can make exceptions, of course, but in that case there has to be something special about the woman. Or else she has to be a professional whore, fully trained and just tough enough, convinced that there's nothing worse in this world than what she's already experienced. To snap that kind of girl like a dry branch is something that demands both determination and imagination. Both qualities I've never lacked.

The couples I was interested in were those who had not "something" but *everything* to hide. The couples that, once they were found out, would lose every last thing they possessed, the ones who truly couldn't afford it. They were hard to flush out, and for the most part they were a waste of time. I'd follow them, gathering information, and then I'd look for a way to enter into their lives with all the delicacy of a medieval *condottiere* taking an enemy castle.

Sometimes blackmail wasn't enough. Then it became necessary to resort to threats, depriving the half of the couple who had the money of the company of the other half. I had put together a little gang. Two brothers, Furio and Toni Centra, failed dental technicians who had gone out of business not only because of the larger financial crisis but also because of their general lack of interest in hard work, held my guests hostage for a reasonable fee in the cellar of their now defunct company. These were very short periods of captivity and none of my targets were taken by force. They all believed that they were going to an appointment where they would finally be able to resolve this extremely unpleasant episode, and instead they soon found themselves bound and gagged. They were treated well, all things considered. The Centra brothers had only gone overboard once, with a woman who owned a perfumery, the wife of a well-known chief physician with outsized ambitions; she was having an affair with another woman who was prominent in hard-right Catholic circles.

Certain that they'd be curing her of her homosexuality, they'd gotten a shade too enthusiastic and it hadn't been easy to hush the matter up.

In spite of the fact that we were able to act with impunity, a product of our victims' guaranteed silence, I'd decided that the Swiss woman and her professor would be our last marks, reasoning that any criminal activity tends to have a short shelf life. And also because, as Italian children like to say, "*il gioco è bello se dura poco*"—"the best games don't last too long." And I was already getting sick of this one. I wanted to move on to something else, though exactly what I wasn't sure. My comfortable economic position allowed me to take my time looking around.

The two of them had come in one night and I'd immediately taken a shine to them. She belonged to that slice of the upper class almost entirely unknown in Veneto. There were just the few prominent families that had controlled most of the land since the time of the Venetian Doges, and eventually ended up in industry, but you'd never find any of them in my restaurant. They knew all about my troubles with Brianese and avoided me. They considered me well beneath their notice.

He, on the other hand, was truly insignificant. He was unassuming in his appearance, dress, and tastes. Once, pouring him a glass of wine from a hundred-euro bottle she had obviously chosen, I'd caught the scent of a cologne he'd applied liberally and which I knew cost half that much. The two of them came from distant universes, fate had brought them together and then set in motion that strange alchemy that made them fall in love and then walk into my restaurant.

Because between the two of them it was true love. Without a doubt. An island of sincere feeling in a dining room full of people who didn't know the meaning of either of those words. Including—especially—me. So I decided that this couple would be the perfect capstone to my brief foray into crimes against illicit lovers.

Two months to gather the necessary information. The weak link was undoubtedly Guido Di Lello.

He surrendered immediately and unconditionally. I intercepted him as he was leaving the university in Venice and showed him, on my cell phone, a picture I'd taken at La Nena.

I invited him to come have an espresso with me, and he followed me like a steer to the slaughter. When I told him that my goal was to relieve his lover of a little of her cash, he heaved a sigh of relief. He was willing to do anything I asked in order to get off scot-free. I had a little fun humiliating him, making him tell me every detail of their relationship, even the most intimate ones.

It was easy to get him to go along with a fake kidnapping. Half a day, at the very most. Oriana would get out her jewels, cross the border, and once she'd handed over the "ransom," he'd go back to living his life.

"Here's a piece of advice," I said as I drove him over to the Centra brothers, who would host him for as long as it would take—obviously much longer than I had promised him. "Forget about secret affairs. You're not built for this kind of complicated relationship, you're too weak and cowardly."

He burst into tears, and I pretended to be surprised.

The plan that I'd considered conceptually perfect was flawlessly implemented, and still it turned into a resounding defeat thanks to one simple fact: the wealthy matron refused to pay the ransom. She simply cut all ties and vanished. She abandoned the man of her dreams to his fate. Those two really were hilarious. They'd sworn undying love, and then each had betrayed the other in the worst possible way without batting an eyelash.

That big Swiss slut needed to be punished. I could have done it by making public her affair with the professor, but that would have attracted the attention of the cops.

Instead I went to see the Centra brothers and ordered them to kill the hostage. A job that was handsomely paid, of course. Furio and Toni were a pair of thoroughly debauched individuals. They had both reached their forties without being able to construct any lasting personal relationships. They devoted their emotional lives to whores, whores they paid for with the cash they always seemed in desperate need of, seeing as they'd never been able to make good use of their skills. Coarse and ignorant, they hated all that was different, all that was foreign to the Venetian boondocks where they lived. Like Guido Di Lello: an intellectual, a Roman, a musician on the side, who didn't even understand dialect and only spoke in proper Italian. The idea of rubbing out this parasite excited them.

I just loved the Centra brothers, monsters who escaped all suspicion, waiting to be shaped and pushed toward unimaginable excesses. Tools as useful as they were expendable. I had met them through an old partner of mine in the prostitution business; she used to arrange for them to enjoy a girl's company once a month. None of the girls wanted to make herself available to those two, and I had to remind them more than once of the rules of their employment. Intrigued by their reputations as filthy swine, one time I accompanied a recalcitrant Dominican prostitute who was going to meet them and instantly sniffed out the rot at their core. I only had to pretend to like them a little, and Furio and Toni soon threw open the abyss of their hearts and minds to me.

Even though more than a year had passed, I still couldn't find the words to describe the way in which the professor had faced his death. He was certainly terrified but there was something in his eyes that suggested he was somehow too dismayed to beg for pity. He was tortured until I finally grew bored with his screams and his suffering. Then they hammered him to death. I convinced the two brothers to bury the corpse in the garden behind the building that had once housed their little operation as dental technicians; that meant I'd have one more chip to bargain with if and when relations between us went south.

I repaid Signora Oriana Pozzi Vitali in the same currency: silence. I was hoping that uncertainty over her lover's fate and a sense of guilt would turn her life into a living hell. Instead, she managed to surprise me a second time by hiring two mercenaries to find out who'd kidnapped and murdered her professor.

I wasn't afraid of them. There was just one thing. After a long search, I'd finally found one last pair of lovers who could adequately make up for the slap in the face I'd taken from that Swiss woman, and before I could move forward I'd have to make sure those two amateur sleuths surrendered, confronted with the fact that there was no way to get to the bottom of what had happened.

Federico Togno showed up around lunchtime. I didn't have any empty tables, so I seated him at the bar. I took care of my customers while he chowed down on *tagliatelle ai funghi*, noodles in a nice mushroom sauce.

A building contractor who wanted to make a good impression on a few clients he'd invited to lunch took me aside and asked me to pick the wines to accompany the meal; money was no object. I took a quick look at what they had ordered so I could get an idea of what would go with what. "It'll cost you about a thousand euros," I informed him, aiming high.

"That's fine. The main thing is I want to make sure that my guests know it."

"Leave that to me."

Once I was done playing the part of a sommelier overjoyed at the chance to finally serve such fine vintages, I managed to get over to my trusted snoop.

"Well?"

"Marco Buratti and Max the Memory. They used to work as unlicensed private detectives," he said, handing me a file folder. "But no one's seen them around here in years. At a certain point they sold off everything they owned and disappeared. Brigadier Stanzani says they're harmless."

As I skimmed the Carabinieri reports I glimpsed a name that gave me a shock: Beniamino Rossini. People who had made an enemy of that man had lived to bitterly regret ever tangling with him.

"Has Rossini been spotted?"

"No. Apparently he lives in Lebanon."

I nodded with satisfaction. Just as well. I could handle those two assholes but their badass friend would be a tough nut to crack even for someone of my caliber.

"Keep following them."

He made a face. "It's Maria José's birthday."

"This is an emergency and it's not as if you're doing me a favor, since I give you a paycheck every month."

"You're right, it's just that my wife was really counting on it and she's going to hold a grudge. You know yourself what women are like."

I smiled. "Put the blame on that heartless bastard of a boss of yours. You'll see, she won't bust your chops."

The phone rang. I immediately recognized the voice that wished to reserve a table. It was the woman of the couple I had in my sights.

"For you, there's always a table, Signora Moscati," I chirped. And then I wondered how she'd come up with that surname as an alibi. Perhaps it was the name of an old schoolmate or a neighbor. I couldn't wait to get the chance to ask.

CHAPTER SEVEN

Three more restaurants and we'd be done with the list the Swiss lady had given us.

"I'm not going to remind you that I warned you," Max said. "In terms of food and wine it's been interesting, but personally I can't wait to get back into the kitchen."

"You're getting old."

He waved his forefinger in my face vehemently. "No. I've reached a degree of maturity in my work at the stove, both theoretically and in practice, so that I feel the need to express myself in my own medium, just as any other artist would."

"You're getting old," I reiterated firmly. "Left-wing radicals in their fifties like you, left behind by history, have all been infected with the cooking virus; it's an epidemic that's spreading faster than Ebola because it's hitting even greater numbers. In fact, like any epidemic, it's cutting across class lines throughout society. Old and young, left-wing and right-wing, women and men, straight and gay, atheists and believers."

"So what?"

I shrugged. "I was just venting," I explained. "After all the crap they've been stuffing us with in these restaurants, I'm feeling a little bloated. Every trend has its observant orthodox ballbusters."

He laid a hand on my shoulder with an affectionate gesture. "To tell the truth, some of them were pretty heavy-handed, trying to palm pompous names, fashionable chefs, over-adventurous wine lists off on us," he whispered, his eyes gleaming.

"Luckily you can count on me and my cuisine, in which the concepts of the regional and the seasonal merge with a bioethical vision of globalization."

I pulled out my cell phone.

"What are you doing?" asked the fat man.

"Making a reservation at Alberto all'Anfora."

My partner raised his hands in a gesture of surrender. "Whatever you say. Let's make it at eight, so we have time to drink a spritz together in the piazza."

Actually, Max went to have a spritz in the piazza alone, because he categorically refused to go with me to meet Campagna in a bar just outside of town that was popular with retirees. The furnishings hadn't been replaced since the seventies, and neither had the bartender behind the bar.

"The white wine's decent here," the cop recommended.

"I don't think you invited me to this out-of-the-way little dive just so I could sample the wine."

"I bought five euros' worth of Indian jujubes and they were soft. This time of the year they ought to be hard and crunchy. The fact is that the heat isn't letting up," he told me, without bothering to reply. "Then the cold air pours down from the north and we get hit with hurricanes, cyclones, and all the crops are ruined. It's always the countryside that pays the price."

"Should I be noticing the pun on your surname, because *la campagna* means the countryside?"

"Certainly. Giulio Campagna, country cop, at your service," he hissed sarcastically.

I stood up. "You certainly know how to try my patience."

At that point he grabbed my arm. "Sit down, Buratti. I need to talk to you."

"As long as you've exhausted your store of bullshit."

He told me to go to hell, waving one hand in the air dismissively. "The other night there was a pretty decent little raid in a local hotel," he began to explain. "My colleagues had come to learn that there was an arrangement between the owners and a ring of escorts who used a certain number of hotel rooms without registering the IDs of the guests. One of these young ladies has a long-standing relationship with a drug dealer who's on the run from the law, so they understandably figured that he too might be making use of this facility to see her.

"No such luck. The woman was there with a traveling salesman from Varese who had made a reservation with her through a website two weeks previous. Now, I ask you: how does a guy know so far ahead and with such precision that fourteen days from now he's going to feel like fucking a professional? Does he have preprogrammed erections?"

I snorted. "I'm not sure I want to investigate the matter."

"You're right, I digress," he admitted as he gestured for another glass of wine. "But in another room we found a young housewife with no criminal record who was entertaining a brigadier with the Carabinieri, a certain Stanzani."

"Should I be shocked?"

"Not so much at the fact that he was with a whore, but maybe at the fact that he conducted an unauthorized background check on you and Max the Memory."

"Are you certain?" I asked, aghast.

"The detective in charge of the operation, who smelled a rat, talked to the brigadier's superior officers and after a quick investigation, it turned out that he had the bad habit of sticking his nose in places it didn't belong, probably on behalf of insurance companies and private investigative agencies. That little unauthorized investigation on you two was the last in a long series."

I took a sip. "Private investigative agencies?"

"The ones that are legit are run by former law enforcement officers who have wisely kept on good terms with their former colleagues," he replied. "But in this case we have no idea who was involved because the carabiniere refuses to talk. He's openly denying concrete facts, just to limit the damage."

I felt the urge for a cigarette and walked outside. It's never a good feeling to find out that someone's been tailing you, but if it turned out that the officer's curiosity was somehow connected to the case of the missing professor, it could still end up being to our advantage.

Campagna tagged after me with a couple of full glasses. "I know what you're thinking. If we can find out who's paying the brigadier, then maybe we can find a connection to the Di Lello kidnapping."

"That's right. We haven't been here long. We've been careful and discreet. We've worked exclusively on this case," I said. "I doubt there are any other explanations."

"And I doubt that a gang at that level would turn to a private detective to find out who you are."

"Then we need to find out who hired the carabiniere."

Campagna snickered. "So are you going to go ask him? Or are you going to send that fat friend of yours?"

"No. That's your job. After all, you're both cops."

"I can't. I already tried once and the big boss ordered me to stay away from him, in person."

"We don't have any other leads to follow up right now."

The cop emptied his glass and clicked his tongue. "This lead is mine and I just told you it doesn't go anywhere at all," he hissed. "You need to earn your keep, Buratti, see if you can't move your ass for a change."

He must have already tossed back three or four glasses of white wine. "Are you drinking on an empty stomach?" I asked, trying to make him feel like an asshole. "Do you want me to order you a panino, to soak up some of the alcohol?"

"How much is the wealthy Swiss matron paying you?"

"Help me understand—is this about money?"

He grabbed my wrist. "Don't you dare. I've never taken so much as a penny in my life."

"Then I don't understand why you keep circling back to the

same subject," I retorted, twisting out of his grip. "This is how I make a living and my rates are none of your business."

Campagna changed the subject and his attitude. By now I'd figured out that this was his way of placating the deep-seated anger that tormented him when he felt frustrated.

"There's no sign of any new gangs," he informed me. "I also went back over all the reports from the day of the kidnapping, I've pestered taxi and bus drivers. I'm seriously starting to believe that Di Lello went willingly to the appointment with his kidnappers."

I pulled my wallet out of my jacket pocket. "You need anything else?"

He shook his head. "This case is starting to piss me off," he said. "I don't want to wind up with an unsolved murder, drinking *ombre* of white wine with you, trying to figure out where we went wrong."

He pointed his finger toward the city. "I can't stand the idea that someone's taking advantage like this. It's one thing to get away with a burglary, a little dope dealing, but we can't let a gang get away with kidnapping and murder. I need to catch them, do you understand that?"

"If you were in my shoes, how would you approach Brigadier Stanzani?"

"They're already selling chestnuts," he snorted in annoyance. "How are you supposed to eat chestnuts in this heat? It really is true what I heard some guy say: 'There's no more spring or fall and Europe died in Sarajevo.'"

I told him to go to hell and paid the tab. When I walked past him he said: "Stanzani isn't corrupt, at least not in the classic sense. He does favors for people he knows, people who stay on the right side of the law, you get me? He'd never go to work for organized crime."

Campagna really was a complicated man.

"I don't follow. What do you mean?"

"If I were in your shoes, which I never would be, I'd tread carefully—but at the same time I'd use a heavy hand."

Tread carefully? Heavy hand? I took a deep breath in order to avoid saying something insulting, and got up to leave without saying goodbye.

"His wife!" he said in a loud voice. "Threaten to tell her everything. I could never pull such a nasty trick on a fellow cop but you're a pretty ruthless guy."

I retraced my steps. "You think that might work?"

"No cop alive is capable of tolerating hell at home, I know that from experience. It's too tough of a job already not to be able to depend on a solid emotional life," he confided, handing me a sheet of paper with all the brigadier's personal information. "When they took Stanzani in, the only thing he asked was that his spouse not be allowed to know a thing. He was more worried about what she might think than about his superior officers."

I drove toward the center of town musing about the best way to break down the carabiniere's defenses without incurring consequences. I didn't want to wind up in an interrogation room facing the third degree for harassing him.

Max was there, in the piazza, sitting at a tableful of fifty-year-olds talking animatedly about politics, cigarettes and drinks in hand. I came up behind him just as he was saying: "We've always been right, but we've always lost. Why?"

I know that phrase like the back of my hand and I knew it was going to lead to an endless and melancholy discussion, whose empty weight was all too familiar to me.

"I'm hungry," I announced, knowing that I was bringing up a valid point. "And our table awaits."

The fat man got to his feet, pulled a rumpled banknote out of his pocket, and slipped it under his empty glass. "I'm going to keep this guy company, he gets depressed when he eats alone."

"Thank God you came along," he whispered the minute we'd moved a safe distance away. "The ineluctable drift of the same old talk was sweeping us inexorably toward a pointless moment of self-awareness."

"Shameless. You were the one directing the choir."

He smiled. "I never can seem to resist the temptation. Though to tell the truth, I can't stop asking myself the same questions, having given so much to the cause."

I thought to myself that the cause had ransacked his life and now no one cared because it was all part of the past.

"What did Campagna tell you?" he asked, lighting himself a cigarette.

I brought him up-to-date, omitting some of the man's more demented tangents to avoid giving him an excuse to speak ill of the police officer.

"That carabiniere is going to get us into deep shit," Max retorted, clearly worried. "We definitely can't just stop him in the street and threaten to get him into trouble with his wife."

"No, you're right, but we can be a little more devious and a little more cunning."

"How?"

"By treading carefully and using a heavy hand, obviously."

Max shot me a stern glare. "Hanging out with that cop is seriously compromising your sanity."

The next morning Signora Mariangela Crema Stanzani went out to the market to do her grocery shopping. We'd been tailing her since she'd left her apartment building and, thanks to the photograph on her Facebook page, we were positive that this was indeed the carabiniere's spouse. A physically robust woman who wasn't averse to taking fashion risks, especially as far as the length of her skirt was concerned.

"She goes to the same boutiques as Campagna," Max joked.

The time had come to see whether the plan I'd worked out had even a ghost of chance. I'd have preferred to call from a phone booth, but these days phone booths were on the verge of extinction and I had to settle for my cell phone.

"*Buongiorno*, Brigadier."

"Who's calling?"

"It's Buratti. You recently conducted an unauthorized background check on me and of a friend of mine."

"And how the fuck do you know about it?" he asked, after a moment's silence.

"From a trusted source: the police," I replied with sincerity. "I'm not interested in getting you into trouble but I do need to know who commissioned your investigation."

"You have no authority to ask me a fucking thing," he snarled nastily. "You and your friend are both ex-convicts, you're jailbirds, you're dangers to society. And don't you ever dare to call me back, or I'll paint your ass black and blue. I'll send you back behind bars so fast . . ."

I decided to cut off that flood of threats and insults. "Your wife is out doing a little grocery shopping. I'll just go over, tap her on the shoulder, and tell her that the cops caught you in bed with a hooker and that you weren't using a condom."

"You'd better stay away from her, plus she'd never believe you."

It only took a few strides for me to reach the woman. "Signora Stanzani."

She turned around, surprised. "Do I know you?"

"No," I replied, handing her the cell phone. "But I just happened to be talking to your husband and I thought you'd like to say hi."

The woman didn't stop at hi; in fact she dragged her husband into a discussion, as grueling as it was pointless, on the need to modify the menu for their Sunday dinner.

"Let's hope that the brigadier gives us the name and that you're not forced to rat him out, because it's a mathematical certainty that that woman will go after you with her purse if you do," Max decreed sagely.

The woman scolded her husband for taking up so much of her time and finally handed my cell phone back to me.

"Buratti?"

"Yes?"

"Don't think you'll get away with this. You can't begin to imagine the mess you've gotten yourself into."

"Are you telling me I need to have a heart-to-heart with your wife?"

"No. I was just trying to give you a glimpse of your future," he explained, his voice shaking with fury.

"The name."

He heaved a sigh. "Federico Togno."

"Who's that?" I asked, surprised. The name meant nothing to me.

"You can find that out on your own, dickhead."

"Your wife is still dangerously within reach."

"He's a former colleague, an ex-cop, you can always find him at La Nena. And anyway, he didn't have it in for you, he just came in to run a license plate and your name popped up."

I hung up. I brought Max up to speed.

"The license plate of the jalopy you just bought," he said.

"Right."

"La Nena?"

"Right."

"Martina and Gemma."

"And Giorgio, the proprietor."

We exchanged a long, hard glance as we both reached the same conclusion. For the first time since we'd taken the case, we could say we'd found a clue. Tenuous, sure, but a clue that nevertheless bore further investigation.

"Are you going to tell Campagna?"

"Not right away. Maybe later."

"He's able to get information much more easily than we can."

"True. But if it turns out to be a solid lead, he'll just take the case away from us," I pointed out.

"So what do we do now?" asked the fat man.

"Let's go get to know this guy Togno."

"We can take it for granted that the carabiniere is going to warn him; when we come face to face with him he'll stick us with some believable whopper."

"Which we're not going to believe, unless we can check it out for ourselves," I concluded in a professional tone of voice.

The ex-carabiniere too had posted his picture on his Facebook page. When you're looking for someone these days, your first stop has to be the social networks. Even a few fugitives from justice who must have been tiring of their precarious freedom couldn't resist finding old and new friends online, and the law had taken advantage to yank them out of circulation.

Max used a fake account, I didn't even want to consider the idea. Not because I was opposed to it on principle or suspicious of the medium for some reason, but simply because I had nothing to share or post. And that wasn't a bad thing.

Togno was at the bar in La Nena, sipping an aperitif. A Negroni, I guessed from the color. Instead of potato chips or peanuts, he was spearing chunks of octopus dripping olive oil and lemon juice. An unusual combination. Giorgio, the proprietor, was chatting with him, but he walked away the moment he saw us enter the restaurant. The ex-carabiniere must have been about forty-five but he looked good for his age; he liked to dress well, though his shoes needed a new pair of heels. His watchful gaze roved the room, searching. Just some guy, or so you'd say if it wasn't for the son-of-a-bitch expression stamped on his face, a snarl that became a smile when I went over and introduced myself.

"Why, of course, Marco Buratti," he repeated, vigorously gripping my hand. "And you must be Max," he added, grabbing the fat man's right hand. "I owe you an apology. I mixed up the first two numbers of the license plate I was interested in, that's all. Can I get you both something?"

He hadn't had time to cook up the plausible lie that Max had taken for granted.

"The car is registered in my name," I pointed out. "Not my friend's name. And yet Brigadier Stanzani extended his investigation to include him."

Togno's face changed expression. "Well, you'll have to ask him about that."

"We already have," Max broke in. "He says that you specifically asked about us both."

"It was just a misunderstanding," the ex-carabiniere said defensively. "I offer you my apologies, I'll buy you a drink, and we can forget it ever happened."

I threw my arms up. "There's a police investigation underway," I lied. "I doubt that the word 'misunderstanding' is going to persuade the police to shelve this case."

Togno retorted in the same key. "In that case, I'll be talking about it with the police, not with you. Now, if the two of you don't mind, I'd like to go back to drinking in blessed peace."

Unhurriedly we each sat on a stool to either side of him and ordered a couple of aperitifs, like two ordinary patrons. A few minutes later, two gentlemen in their sixties walked in the front door—they were well dressed and clearly had plenty of money. The proprietor rushed to welcome them.

"*Caro* Pellegrini, as you can see we've come back to enjoy some more of your excellent cuisine," one of the two men said loudly, in a voice whose inflections were unmistakably Emilian.

Max's reaction was sudden and reckless. He clutched my shoulder until it hurt and said in an even louder voice: "Giorgio Pellegrini!"

The restaurateur turned around. He and Max stared at each other for a few seconds. I knew my friend and was certain that his glance contained a clear look of contempt. The fat man put down his glass and headed for the exit without another word. I paid the check and followed.

I caught up with him in the beautiful piazza not far away as he was taking a seat at a table outside another bar.

"What the fuck just came over you?"

"Giorgio Pellegrini," he repeated the name in a grim voice. "Now I understand who he is. I've heard plenty of rumors about him."

"Do you mind telling me too?"

Max said nothing, grabbed his phone, and pulled up train schedules. "There's a train in an hour. I've just got time to bolt a meal."

"Where are you headed?"

"Milan."

We were interrupted by the waitress. The fat man ordered enough food for three people his size. An obvious sign of the anxiety that was weighing him down at that moment.

"I'm going to have to dive back into the past," he explained after devouring the first panino. "I have to go see certain people who know the owner of La Nena very well."

"And that's the last thing you feel like doing."

"We've never liked each other. And now less than ever."

"No one's forcing you to do this."

He gulped down the dark beer greedily. "But I really have to," he retorted, but said nothing more. He shut himself up in an uneasy silence until it was time to head to the station.

"I may be gone a few days," he said.

"You know where to find me."

On the way to the parking lot I took the long way so I could pass by La Nena. I stopped at the entrance to peer inside. It was still warm enough out to leave the front door wide open.

The restaurant was packed. Giorgio Pellegrini was fluttering from table to table with his usual charming smile. At a certain point he saw me and for a moment he was faced with my curiosity. His expression remained unchanged. Only his eyes were suddenly different. They were devoid of any trace of humanity.

CHAPTER EIGHT

That asshole Buratti thought he could scare me by standing there at the entrance with his hands in his pockets. He was staring at me with that face of his, like an alcoholic bluesman's. His buddy was nowhere in sight. Maybe, after recognizing me, he went home to think back over our shared history. Max the Memory. An aging relic of those years who now must spend his Saturday nights with all the other losers, playing Risk and insulting the government. Bunch of pathetic failures.

I had to wait until I knew that all my guests had been served and satisfied before I could make my way over to the bar where that idiot Federico Togno was waiting for me, looking like a beaten dog.

"What the fuck have you done now?" I asked, keeping a lid on my urge to shout. "Why on earth did those two come into my place looking for you?"

The stooge told me the whole story, down to the smallest details. A mixture of bad luck, random chance, and sheer stupidity was now seriously threatening to focus police attention on Togno, though he knew nothing at all about what had happened to the professor. Buratti and his beer-bellied buddy, who actually were on the trail of the late academic, might suspect something, in part thanks to the bad reputation I enjoyed in certain circles.

The situation was well under control, but I had enough experience to know that underestimating what had happened might be the equivalent of handing myself over to the law. Details apparently devoid of significance can pile up on top of a mountain, until suspicions transform them into an avalanche that suddenly breaks loose and roars down into the valley. It was necessary to react promptly, with a Plan A and a Plan B. Plan A, strictly tactical, was designed to confuse the enemy and ward off suspicion. Plan B was strategic in nature, and should be implemented only if things really went south. Plan A and Plan B. That's why I never really risked having to pay the piper for my crimes.

I gestured for Togno to follow me into the little private dining room that I once used to reserve for Brianese and his herd of corrupt hangers-on. It was bug-proof.

"This is your fault, Federico," I said, attacking him in a harsh voice.

"You're mistaken, I didn't do anything wrong."

"Oh no? Your brigadier wound up right in the middle of a nice raid because you sent him to the wrong hotel."

"How could I have known that was going to happen?" the idiot stammered.

"You're paid to know things like that."

"Okay, so I made a mistake," he said, fumbling for the right words. "But I don't see why you're so angry about it. After all, nothing serious has happened, the whole thing is going to be covered up, no one wants to get Brigadier Stanzani in trouble."

"Then you tell me why those two assholes found out about your investigation from the police."

"I have no idea, but I already told you: there's not going to be any investigation."

"Maybe not, but those two aren't going to stop buzzing around you."

"Around *me*?" he asked in surprise. "Let them. I don't have anything to hide."

I grabbed him by the chin and forced him to look at me. "You don't have the kind of job that could explain your lifestyle, you commit illegal acts, and you've committed a murder," I reminded him. "You need to get the fuck out from underfoot."

"And how?"

I let go of him. "I'm thinking that over right now. When the time comes, I'll tell you what to do."

Federico Togno, red-faced, mumbled out a farewell and hurried away. After a quick look around, I went over and took a seat at the table where Martina and Gemma were finishing their meal. My wife was looking enviously at the pudding her friend was sampling with gusto. She would have liked to order one for herself, but no waiter in the place would have dreamed of bringing her the dessert. I'd been very specific on that point, since I decided day by day exactly what my wife would be having at each meal.

"What appointments does Martina have this afternoon?" I asked Gemma.

"Pilates at 4:30 and a massage at 6."

"Go pick her up at 4:15," I demanded.

Gemma nodded grimly. That meant she'd be forced to wander around town until then, since I clearly wanted her to stay out of the house.

My spouse, who had understood perfectly exactly what I had in mind, objected under her breath that she had just finished eating, but faced with my complete disinterest, she gave up insisting.

I locked arms with her and we strolled home. The whole way, she wouldn't stop talking. She knew that right then she was allowed to talk all she liked and she took advantage of the opportunity to tell me all about the problems her mother was experiencing as she faced widowhood. I listened to all those trite phrases hoping that fate and old age would soon put an end to my mother-in-law's suffering.

Once we got home, Martina hurried into the bedroom, while I headed into a room that was furnished with only a beautiful armchair upholstered in oxblood-red leather and a spinning bike. I got comfortable and a few seconds later my wife came in, dressed only in a pair of gleaming white panties and climbed onto the bike, awaiting my command: "Spinning, baby, spinning."

She started pedaling and before long she'd found the correct rhythm. I closed my eyes and, lulled by the noise of well-oiled gears, I was finally able to focus on my plans. Buratti, Max the Memory, Togno. I could see their faces clearly, I could hear their voices, and I moved them around like pawns, placing them in a given situation so I could test the results and predict any collateral damage.

The lucidity of those moments was priceless, and it allowed me to see that the whole operation had somehow been compromised and that Plan B would have to be developed much further.

I snapped my fingers and she picked up the pace. I planned my moves, I arranged them carefully. I was ready.

And I was satisfied. I opened my eyes and looked at my spouse. Sweat was streaming down her body, her hair was matted to her head. Complete physical collapse was imminent.

I helped her off the bike and laid her down on the wall-to-wall carpeting. I ripped off her panties and yanked open her legs.

Martina welcomed me gratefully.

CHAPTER NINE

I gulped down a pizza with a couple of beers, well aware that digesting that mess would be no walk in the park. But I didn't feel like sitting alone in a restaurant and that had seemed like the quickest solution. On my way back from the bathroom I spotted a rumpled copy of *Il Mattino* and between bites I leafed through the newspaper's entertainment pages. That was how I found out that soon, in a local club, my old friend Maurizio Camardi, a renowned saxophonist as well as a connoisseur of beautiful women, would be performing with Marco "Ponka" Ponchiroli, a first-rate pianist I'd gone to hear many times before.

The pizzeria didn't stock Calvados so I settled for a grappa. I was worried about Max, who was rummaging around in a part of his past that, despite his efforts, he seemed incapable of letting go. The fat man had an unhappy relationship with the man he had once been. On the one hand, he tried desperately to translate those experiences into something positive in the present; on the other, he struggled to stave off the excesses and the filth that had muddied his dreams and those of many others.

It was the right night to drink more than usual but I decided to stay within the bounds of a sobriety only slightly distorted by alcohol. A formula of my own invention that corresponded to a precise number of small glasses. The fact was that, for a while now, whenever I got drunk I started thinking about Ninon and crying. I missed her and when I imagined her in another man's arms I couldn't hold back my tears.

I let my eyes range over the women sitting at the tables. I

felt so alone and the yearning to love and be loved in return was so violent that I couldn't arrive at any sort of objective selection. The time had come to ask for the check.

I had to wait twenty minutes or so before I could say goodbye to Maurizio. He was busy giving advice to the umpteenth young man who just couldn't seem to win some girl's heart.

"You ought to teach a course in seduction. It would be the most popular class in town," I said as we hugged.

"You aren't the first person to suggest this radical new direction, but I think I'll just stick to music."

Then he asked me if was back in Padua for good. I told him that I didn't know yet. "There comes a time when it's really hard to pick where to live."

"The secret is to never stop traveling," he said, pointing to his sax. "This guy takes me everywhere, which makes coming home a pleasure."

Jazz. I let the good music fill my ears. Every so often I'd check my cell phone, waiting in vain for a message or call from Max.

Around midnight I went back to the two lovers' apartment. It was quiet and it smelled good. I turned on the lights in every room so I could take a good look at the place in bright light, then I undressed and flopped down onto the sofa, ready to binge watch some television.

Those days I obsessively watched absurd programs that told the story of the financial meltdown in the United States. Pawnshops in cities that were economically fucked like Detroit, with endless lines of African-Americans trying to sell anything they could lay their hands on for a few bucks. Houses and mansions were sold off in foreclosure auctions, the dueling buyers attacking each other like sharks, and eventually becoming reality TV characters. Long lines of self-storage units whose padlocks were lopped off with metal shears. The buyers had five minutes to take a look from outside, then they squared off, bids escalating at fifty dollars a pop, vying to purchase objects that had been part of the lives of other people, people who had one day found themselves unable to pay their storage rental fees.

It was impossible not to marvel at the sheer tawdriness of the content, yet something drove me to keep watching. Especially the shows set in the pawnshop world. Women trying to raise bail money to get their men out of jail, forced to reconcile themselves to the fact that they wouldn't be able to do so because their jewelry, television sets, computers, and fur coats were valued at a pittance.

Every so often someone would come in who was just trying to pay for his medication, but that I couldn't stand to watch, so I'd change the channel.

There was a period when I'd kill time until sleep came by pigging out on TV shopping shows. Now the television landscape offered something better: a voyeuristic tour of poverty in the great land of America. The message was always the same: "Go fuck yourselves. It's up to you to pay the costs of the great recession."

The next morning, for no particular reason, I decided to grow out my mustache. It just seemed like a good idea and I looked forward to the day with a mild surge of enthusiasm. I got in my car and headed for La Nena, where I planned to have breakfast, both to mark my territory and to annoy Pellegrini and Togno. When I got there, I found neither. I leafed through a newspaper and sated my hunger with a cappuccino and a pastry, which the menu informed me would cost an arm and a leg. As always, the place was packed with people chatting, laughing, making deals. Five bejeweled ladies were seated near me, intently attacking a tray of *tramezzino* sandwiches and a bottle of pinot grigio. After exhausting the unusual September weather as a subject, they moved on to parish priests. To my surprise they favored a changing of the guard, the advent of a younger generation. They were sick and tired of old priests with backward ideas about separation and divorce and as I listened it became clear that each of them could boast of one or more controversial cases in their own families.

But at a certain point the youngest supplied the boundaries delimiting this group's concept of change. "Just so long as some fresh-faced young priest straight out of the seminary doesn't come along and decide to welcome a herd of Roma into the parish church or else organize a used clothing drive for convicts," she said, to a chorus of approval. "I mean, already nobody seems to know what this new pope has in mind."

I would gladly have continued following this debate, but just then the proprietor made his entrance. Pellegrini noticed me almost instantly, and came over to my table flaunting an exaggerated smile, far too big given the degree of our acquaintance.

"I'm so happy you've come in to sample our breakfasts. Every ingredient is carefully selected," he said in a jovial voice.

"I certainly hope so, considering the prices you charge," I thought to myself, returning his smile.

"Your friend decided not to come?"

"No, not today."

He moved closer and lowered his voice. "The fact that you've come back means that yesterday's unfortunate incident has already been forgotten, right?"

"Certainly," I replied, doing my best to be convincing.

I couldn't pull it off. Pellegrini made that clear to me by shooting me an icy glance.

He turned on his heel and headed straight for the table where the ladies were dining, cheerfully scattering compliments on their outfits, handbags, hairstyles, and makeup, provoking ecstatic reactions. The man had a way about him. He was a true professional when it came to coddling customers. While I was paying the check, an attractive woman of about thirty-five, drinking an espresso at the counter, started staring at me and smiling in a manner that was extremely discreet but also unmistakable. I smiled back just long enough to figure out she was a housewife who was hooking on weekday mornings, when she was free from family obligations. I waved goodbye and headed out the door to my Škoda, which waited faithfully in the parking lot.

But I'd gone less than fifty yards when I ran into Gemma, who was walking wearily and with a bored expression.

"Breakfast at La Nena, I'll bet," she said without bothering to say hello.

"That's right. And you're going in for breakfast now?"

She checked the time on her cell phone. "Yes, well, actually I'm killing time until Martina's done with her zumba class."

"You two are inseparable," I said, not thinking.

She decided to have some fun with me. "We live together, in fact," she explained, staring at me. "Her, me, and Giorgio."

My curiosity piqued, I accepted the challenge. "A ménage à trois?"

"There's nothing wrong with that, don't you agree?"

"Nothing at all." I decided that she wanted to chat and that maybe she could give me some information about Togno, since she and Pellegrini's wife spent so much time in the restaurant.

"Can I treat you to an espresso, Gemma?" I asked, using her given name for the first time.

"Gladly," she replied, without a second's hesitation. "It's been quite a while since another man invited me to spend a little time with him."

"You're living in a relationship that's become too exclusive."

She broke into a forced laugh that clearly revealed the mask this melancholy woman hid behind, devastated as she was by a complicated existence she didn't seem at all proud of.

She linked arms with me and walked me to a very unpretentious café overlooking a piazza crowded with stalls.

She ordered a glass of red wine and a couple of meatballs.

She'd get along famously with Max. I settled for a glass of prosecco.

"I'd recognized him, you know?" she said suddenly.

"Who?"

"The man in the picture you showed to me and Martina. Professor Di Lello."

"Had you seen him at La Nena?"

"Plus on TV, and in the papers. I'm a girl who likes to keep up with the news, you know?"

"But you didn't say anything the other night."

"At La Nena discretion is the first rule, and the second, and the third."

"Giorgio said that he didn't remember him."

"Neither did Martina," she replied in an ambiguous tone of voice. Then she ordered seconds on wine and meatballs. She didn't kid around in the morning either.

I wanted to ask her about Togno but there was something unsettling about that woman that kept me from dismissing her entirely.

"You don't take care of yourself the way your girlfriend does," I said frankly, pointing to her plate and glass.

She snickered. "I'm the lady's companion. I can't be perfect, quite the opposite. My defects have to be as evident as possible, to please my lord and his lady."

I stared at her, trying to gauge if she was serious. She smiled and tapped me sharply on the hand. "I'm only kidding."

"Do you know Federico Togno?" I asked. "He's always hanging around at La Nena."

She didn't answer. "Why are you and that fat friend of yours looking for the professor?"

I took the time I needed to construct an adequate answer, certain that every word I said would be reported back to Pellegrini.

"There's a person who's suffering and can't seem to put her heart at rest, and she's asked us to help her."

"His sweetheart?"

I avoided the question. "The tragedy of being forced to live without news of a person you love is a terrible thing, and in time it becomes intolerable. There's nothing that can alleviate that suffering. Nothing."

Gemma grabbed her glass. "Not even this?" she asked, trying to quiet the anxiety I'd provoked in her.

I wasn't trying to be cruel, but I kept after her. I was precise and detailed, feeling sure I'd be able to break through her armor of self-destructive cynicism. Toward the end, I asked her once more about Togno.

She didn't answer this time either. She preferred to slip into ambiguity, her favorite territory.

"Giorgio is a king of hearts," she said. "What kind of king are you?"

"Maybe I don't want to be a king at all," I replied at random.

She shook her head in disappointment and started to get up. I took her hand.

"Can I give you my cell phone number?"

"What for?" she asked warily.

"Maybe you'll feel like calling me sometime."

"All you want from me is answers," she retorted bitterly. "There's nothing else you're interested in."

It was the right time to lie to her. Gemma was ready to believe anything as long as I made her think I was attracted to her.

Instead I remained silent. That woman was strange and unhappy, she deserved respect. In my world there was no such thing as a lady's companion.

She picked up her cell phone and entered my number, then left the café with her head down. She stopped to dry her eyes and light a cigarette. I followed her to a building in the center of town that housed the gym where Martina went to stay in shape. When Martina emerged, Gemma greeted her with a smile and told her something that made her laugh. They walked together, stopping to look at shop windows, then they went into La Nena.

Max called toward evening. "I'm coming back on the last train. Make sure there's something for me to eat."

I was the least suitable person imaginable to entrust with the task of satisfying a fat man with culinary pretentions. I hurried out to the finest deli in the neighborhood where I was advised by a woman whose only fault lay in her portions, which tended to be overlarge.

After a quick sprint over to the wine shop I headed home and killed time drinking spritzes and watching TV. While channel surfing I happened upon a show about medical cases that featured the story of a sixteen-year-old boy who weighed 675 pounds. His mother, scarred by the death of her first child, stuffed her second-born like a French goose, until he eventually turned into a statue made of lard, partially reclining under a canopy. To save his life, with the financial assistance of the television network, they finally rushed him to the hospital in a fire engine and there he became, for all intents and purposes, a body to be snipped at, weighed, and displayed whenever the opportunity arose. His mother kept bringing him "a little something" to snack on, but since she was a cast member, no one dared to shoo her away much less banish her.

I changed the channel when it became evident that that kid had no chance of ever leading a normal life again. The TV crew had showed up too late.

A fucked-up story, but one I couldn't stop thinking about as I walked toward the train station. That night I wanted to keep my mind free of all thoughts until Max returned.

My friend and partner stepped off the train, mopping his forehead with a handkerchief. "Of course, the air conditioning wasn't working," he said, plunging into a ferociously articulate jeremiad against the management of the Italian railroads.

"So what did you find out?" I asked abruptly.

He gestured for me to offer him a cigarette. "Sorry," he muttered, "I'm a little shook up."

"Pellegrini?"

"A real piece of shit," he decreed. "He was a member of one of the splinter groups in the larger solar system of freebooters in the armed political struggle, but then one day he and a partner set off a bomb and by mistake blew up a security guard who was about to retire, an old guy just making his rounds on a bicycle.

"The only thing left for them to do was to run, and the two of them soon found themselves carrying AK-47s in the ranks of a liberation movement in a country in Central America. I'm skipping over lots of details, but soon his young lordship got tired of the struggle and went back to Europe alone, because his comrade had met a bad end. First he stopped in Paris, where he announced that he had absolutely no intention of paying his debt to society, and then went on to openly blackmail his old comrades: either they were going to find a diehard militant already serving life without parole who'd be willing to cop to the crimes he was accused of, or he'd testify against everyone who was still walking around free, whether innocent or guilty.

"The others gave in of course, and he turned himself in at the border. He got off with a short stint in prison, where he distinguished himself by his disgraceful behavior, but he failed to hold up his end of the bargain after all, and named all the people he'd promised to protect to the DIGOS. And even though none of them actually wound up behind bars, they all found themselves forced to at least make a show of collaborating with the police. Luckily for them, it was all over by then, the organization no longer existed, and after a couple of years they were left alone."

I was stunned. It was hardly news that some had avoided prison by blackmailing the people with whom they'd once shared dreams and decisions, but it was clear that Pellegrini had the background and the skill set to lead the gang of lovers, or the gang that was kidnapping them anyway. There was no concrete proof, but by now I felt sure of it.

"It's him," I said.

"Yes," Max agreed. "In Milan, in great secrecy, they introduced me to one of their trusted lawyers, and he told me that he'd run into Pellegrini while defending a member of the Maltese mafia. Apparently Pellegrini had been implicated in a prostitution and human trafficking ring, but suddenly his name disappeared from the investigator's files."

"Friends in high places."

"Sante Brianese," my partner confirmed. "Now he's fallen into disgrace but the attorney in question helped handsome Giorgio to clean up his image and open La Nena."

"Costly operations," I commented. "It's fair to wonder where he found the cash."

We lit two more cigarettes and smoked in silence as we walked through the streets in the center of town.

"We need a plan," I said suddenly, thinking that what we really needed was old Rossini and his pistols.

"Right. But first we need to eat. Good ideas stay far away from empty stomachs."

On Corso Milano, a line of cars was parked alongside the porticoes onto which shops and bars looked out. At that hour, they were all closed. A man emerged from the shadows, his face wrapped in a scarf, his right arm extended, his right hand gripping a pistol.

"He's got a gun!" shouted Max as he lunged at me and shoved me to one side.

Two shots rang out and a second later my friend's oversized body slid to the ground. The stranger fired again but these shots missed their mark. Then he took off, vanishing down a narrow side street.

I leaned over the fat man. He was moaning in pain and losing a lot of blood from his back and side. I felt as if I was losing my mind because I couldn't manage to move a muscle. I was petrified. Max needed help and I was standing there reliving a very similar scene from years ago, when the body hitting the ground, riddled with the bullets of hit men sent by the crime families of the Brenta river basin, belonged to Marielita, his woman. She had died in my arms under a portico in Marostica and I couldn't bear it all happening again.

"Get me some help, Marco," Max spurred me on in a faint voice, and I finally reacted.

"Of course, of course," I stammered as I rummaged for my cell phone. "Don't you worry, you'll see, everything will turn out fine."

"That's what they say in the movies, in real life that's all just bullshit," he retorted, exasperated, before losing consciousness.

"There, now he's dead," I thought to myself as I did my best to get an operator at the emergency hotline to understand me as I frantically told him what had happened.

A three-man squad car showed up first. "It looks like he's still alive," said one police officer, as the other two checked my ID and searched me.

"So what happened?" asked the squad chief.

"Some guy. He wanted to rob us," I lied. "Then for no reason at all he just started shooting."

The third cop started peppering me with questions until I lashed out. "You leave me alone," I shouted, pointing at Max. "Can't you see how badly he's hurt?"

The cop grabbed me by the collar. "If there's any chance of catching him, it's right now, while he's trying to get out of the area," he hissed at me. "But we need to know who we're looking for."

I shot a glance at Max, flat on the ground, motionless, and I took a deep breath. "His face was covered up, he was dressed in dark clothing," I started to tell him. "He demanded our money, he spoke Italian, I didn't see him shooting because my friend protected me. He shielded me with his body, you get that? He got between me and the shooter and took the bullets himself, now do you see?"

The policeman finally realized I was in a state of shock. He went back to the squad car and placed a call to headquarters. Max was still unconscious, but the cop who was crouching beside him kept checking his jugular and continued to reassure me that Max was still with us. I believed him, more or less. I still had Marielita before my eyes, the way her life fled through her lips in the blink of an eye. I'd loved her too, and once we'd even wound up in bed together, but I'd never had the courage to say that to my partner. Maybe he'd guessed but had decided to let it slide: even the strongest friendships can crumble under the weight of words.

Marielita was a woman who was easy to fall in love with. She was a street musician who had been the fat man's eyes and ears for all the years when he was in constant hiding because there was a warrant out for his arrest. I'd never dreamed of stealing her away from him; sex with her had simply been a chance occurrence, if a wonderful one, an affair I was certain would have no aftermath. But her death had left a legacy of questions without answers. At last the siren announced the arrival of medical assistance. After a few minutes Max was strapped to the ambulance gurney and I found myself sitting beside him, observing the pallor of his face in the cruel light of the ambulance's interior, a light that picked out every detail.

"How is he?" I asked in a thin voice.

"We're almost there," a woman replied in a weary tone; she was bundled into a uniform that was a couple of sizes too large.

Max was admitted as a code red, which meant he was in critical condition, and I found myself sitting in a waiting room packed with people. As I watched a girl talk on her cell phone, updating her family on her grandmother's condition, it dawned on me that I still hadn't told anyone what had happened. Actually, there was only one person I'd have wanted to tell, one person whose help I desperately needed, but Beniamino's cell phone was out of range or turned off.

I called Christine Duriez on a number that we'd agreed was only to be used in case of an emergency; I was pretty sure that she was in contact with old Rossini, who had been living the life of a retired robber from the sixties since Sylvie's death. France was the perfect place for that.

She picked up on the ninth ring. "*Oui, Marco?*"

"Someone shot Max. He's in surgery now."

"Where are you?"

"In Padua. Where's Beniamino?"

"Not here."

The woman from Marseille hung up. She'd pass the message on and there was no point wasting time in idle chitchat.

Right then I needed to drink Calvados, listen to blues, and take a few hours off. None of that would be happening though, and the cold fluorescent lights made it seem as if I was already at the morgue.

I got up to find a place outside where I could smoke a cigarette and walked straight into three guys who were heading for me wearing the pissed-off expressions you tend to get when you've just been rudely rousted out of bed.

"DIGOS intelligence service. You're coming with us to police headquarters," they announced.

"DIGOS?" I repeated, aghast. "What do you guys have to do with what happened tonight?"

The three of them exchanged a glance. The sharpest looking member of the trio finally spoke.

"You and the guy clinging to life in the other room have served time for terrorism and now you're surprised that we came down to pick you up?"

because, in any case, you're still a criminal to be prosecuted. I'm seriously considering dedicating my time and energy to putting you behind bars for a good long time."

"You're starting to annoy me," I retorted drily.

"There hadn't been any gunfire in Padua for a while," Campagna persisted. "Brawls between gangs of dope dealers are an everyday occurrence. They massacre each other with broken bottles, with crowbars. Every so often there's a knife, but they set firearms aside for special occasions, because they're noisy and because the cops don't like them.

"But now you two assholes show up for a nice, discreet investigation, and in less than a month someone decides to shoot the two of you dead."

"That doesn't mean that we've broken the law in any way," I retorted, immediately regretting the bullshit I'd just spouted.

The cop reacted immediately, throwing a penholder with the Padua team colors on it straight at me. "Don't push it," he admonished. "You used me and then went out on your own, concealing information from me, and as a result we still don't know if your partner's going to survive."

I raised my voice. "You're the one who told me you couldn't go any further. Obviously, we scared someone so badly that they decided it was worth killing us, but I couldn't tell you who. I haven't kept anything from you."

"Bullshit," he hissed. "You lie with every breath. If you won't talk, I can't help you."

I didn't have the slightest intention of talking. Those two bullets lodged in Max's body had irretrievably altered the trajectory of that case. I threw open my arms. "You have to believe me, all we did is ask around."

"Who did you ask?"

I decided to bring him up to speed on what he was bound to find out anyway. "Brigadier Stanzani, who told us the name of his client, a certain Federico Togno. Who in turn explained to us that it was a regrettable misunderstanding, the result of a mistake in the transcription of a license plate number."

"Bullshit," the cop rapped out. "He asked for information about Max the Memory too, and he doesn't even own a car. Togno provided Brigadier Stanzani with a picture he took with his cell phone and in your file there are plenty of shots of the two of you together. What else?"

"That's it."

"So you're trying to convince me that the key figure is this Federico Togno?"

"Maybe he's somebody else's henchman."

"There was a time when I wanted to get out of this business," Campagna started to tell me, looking out the window as dawn began breaking through the night, "and move to Berlin to follow my dreams: I wanted to open an official embassy for the Venetian *tramezzino*, the best sandwich on earth because it's the softest and the most flavorful. The *tramezzino* contains the quintessential flavors of this land.

"I'd already designed the sign with the name in a type that merged with the silhouette of a gondola. But most importantly, I'd already persuaded my wife and daughter to change everything, move to a new country, learn a new language. And then Wikipedia ruined everything."

I couldn't believe that Campagna had decided to trap me in his office to tell me another one of his nutty stories. "How?" I asked, trying to get him to come to the point.

He held up the index and middle fingers of his right hand. "For two reasons. First, the *tramezzino* isn't Venetian at all, but was first served in a bar in Turin in 1925. There was little or nothing about it that was original, because it was really just an interpretation of the English tea sandwich."

"And the second reason?"

"The name *tramezzino* was invented by D'Annunzio. And frankly I've always thought he was a pain in the ass."

"I'm really sorry about the bad hand that fate dealt you, but I can't quite see what the fuck it has to do with me."

"It means that you told the cops that it was a robbery, but you forgot that I work armed robberies, so now the case is mine. I'm going to be on your ass from now on, with my boss's blessing."

I sighed ostentatiously. "Can I go now?"

"You'll have to come back to sign the transcript of your interview, which I have no intention of bothering to write just now."

"Okay."

"Are you going to the hospital to see Max the Memory?"

"Yes."

"Then I'll come with you."

"There's no need."

He stood up and grabbed his jacket. "No one will even speak to you; you're not a relative and you know how things work here: as soon as they see two people of the same gender, they clam up, just for the fun of it."

Campagna's badge worked miracles. I managed to get a glimpse of Max through a sheet of plate glass in the intensive care ward while a young female surgeon briefed me on his condition.

"The problem isn't so much with bullets—we removed those without complications—but rather your friend's extremely poor cardiac and metabolic condition. He had a heart attack while we were prepping him for the operation and we were forced to perform an angioplasty with the insertion of two stents."

"Will he survive?" the cop asked.

"Yes, but it's going to take time," the surgeon replied. Then she pulled a plastic bag out of her pocket; in it were the two bullets. She gave the bag to Campagna.

".22 caliber. Just like the shells my colleagues found," the inspector declared as soon as the doctor had left. "How far away was that guy when he opened fire?"

"At least ten feet," I replied, thinking back on what had happened.

"It's the kind of handgun used by mafia killers and the intelligence agencies for close-range executions. You place the barrel behind the victim's ear, or against his temple or his heart, and you pull the trigger," he explained. "It certainly isn't well suited for this kind of ambush."

"I don't think he was a professional," I shot back. "For that matter, only his first two shots were good, after that, thankfully, he missed, even though we weren't moving."

"But that contradicts the idea of a gang of badass professionals," the detective noted. "Though the killer operated in the only area near your house that isn't covered by security cameras, and that's an element that suggests intelligence and efficiency. He fired and then turned and ran, heading down a side street where in all likelihood an accomplice was waiting for him at the wheel of a car. If you ask me, they're trying to pull our leg, or better yet, bamboozle us, as an old head of the Mobile Squad used to say."

"What's your plan?"

"You're the last person I'd dream of telling," he said brusquely.

I put a hand on his shoulder. "Thanks."

"For what?"

"For coming here with me."

Campagna shrugged and walked off.

I turned to look at Max. His chest was heaving laboriously with each breath. He was alive. Now I had to face off with Pellegrini and his accomplices and settle this matter; if I tried it alone it would be suicide.

"Please, Beniamino, come back," I sighed, under my breath.

was the fulcrum of Plan B, and if I found it necessary to put that plan in motion, she would have to be in my hands already.

For the first time I found myself experiencing extreme tension. That was all right. I could smell danger and as always in these cases I was preparing to face it head on without the slightest flicker of fear. I didn't know what fear was, and it meant nothing to me. I was the one others were afraid of.

I left the restaurant and went home to see how Gemma was doing. After she'd boasted that she had let Buratti try to pick her up and that she now had his cell phone number, I'd subjected her to a "session" that was a little more severe than usual, and she still hadn't managed to get out of bed. I wasn't a bit worried about her condition, only about the negative effect on Martina's daily routine. All it took was a trifle and my wife, flustered by negative thoughts, would lose the rhythm of her commitments. Her sin was falling victim to continual imperfections. I couldn't afford that.

Gemma was dozing when I walked into her bedroom. The shutters were half closed and there was an unpleasant smell in the air. I threw open the windows and the sun streamed aggressively into the room.

"Leave me alone, King of Hearts," she muttered, covering her eyes with her hands. "You've been bad."

I ripped off the light duvet and sheet and tossed them into the air, then I ripped off her nightgown. "Now I'm going to give you a thorough examination," I announced, pressing a finger on one of her bruises.

Her face twisted with pain. "Please don't."

"Well then I guess you're fine and all you need is a good scrubbing," I said, pulling her by the hair and dragging her to the tub. I grabbed a tube of body wash and squirted it all over her. Then I started rinsing her off with the shower spray turned on full.

"It's freezing," she objected.

"You want it scalding?"

Gemma immediately understood what would happen to her if she insisted and fell silent. She submitted without a peep even when I gave her a good hard scrubbing with a brush. She held her breath when I ran the long wooden handle between her legs.

I threw a towel in her face. "Go get Martina at the gym."

"I'm not sure I can do that," she confessed through her tears.

I huffed in annoyance and opened the medicine chest to get what I needed to give her an injection of painkiller. I took my time preparing it, then I made her turn around and I stabbed the needle into the cheek of her ass.

"Today you're going to have a great big helping of tripe for lunch," I announced before leaving.

Gemma hated tripe. I'd have gladly eaten at their table to keep from missing the show.

When I got back to La Nena a waitress pointed out a guy in a Hawaiian shirt, sitting at a table and boldly staring at the customers.

"A cop," I guessed, but before confronting him, I ordered a smoothie. The guy had asked for an espresso, and he had just barely tasted it.

"Does it not meet with your satisfaction?" I asked in a professional voice. "We can make something else for you, if you wish."

He emptied the demitasse at a single gulp. "It's very good," he said. "I was just distracted because there's something puzzling me—maybe I can ask you if you're the owner of this place."

I stuck out my hand. "Giorgio Pellegrini. La Nena belongs to me."

"Inspector Giulio Campagna, Padua police headquarters, robbery division."

"A pleasure," I said curtly. "What did you want to ask me?"

The cop took his time. "My colleagues tell me that Federico Togno spends all his time in this restaurant and yet nobody seems to have heard of him. Doesn't that strike you as odd?"

I smiled and sat down. "That's because La Nena is an exceptionally discreet restaurant and the staff is following my specific instructions."

"So my colleagues are right?"

"Yes."

"And has he been by today?"

"This morning."

"And since then?"

I pretended to take a look around. "Right now, I don't see him."

The cop peered at the time on his cell phone. I can't stand people who've given up watches in favor of checking the time on their screens. But then what else could you expect from a jerk who sported such a ridiculous shirt in a high-class dining establishment like La Nena? I'd have gladly wiped him off the face of the earth just to punish him for his terrible taste.

"Maybe he'll be back for lunch," the cop ventured.

"Maybe. But why don't you call him? Did you try his house? Or his cell phone?"

"His wife says he went out early this morning, and his cell phone is turned off," he replied with a snicker. "Do you know him well?"

"As well as any restaurateur can know a loyal customer."

"Yes or no?" Campagna pressed.

"Only superficially, as I was trying to explain."

"Because there's another thing I don't understand," the cop continued. "Which is, how does he make his living? He doesn't have a job, the tax office has no records on him, and yet he has a house and a car . . . His wife doesn't work, she's a housewife. He has plenty of bills to pay on a regular basis and yet he seems to live very comfortably. Have you ever given any thought to the question?"

"In my life, I've learned to mind my own business, and I can't tell you how much it's helped me."

"Was that before or after you went to prison?"

I snorted in irritation and looked at him. "I served my time and paid my debt to society, and now I'm a citizen like any other."

"Sante Brianese gave you a hand. In fact, you might say that you owe him everything."

I decided that the time had come to stop being polite and stood up. "The espresso is on the house," I said as I went back to work.

The cop sat in silence and didn't move. After a while he started chatting with someone, then he moved on to someone else. He left his table a little while before lunch began serving, but didn't go far from my restaurant. While Gemma was gulping down her tripe in consommé with tears streaking her face, I saw Campagna pacing back and forth in front of the entrance, his eyes scanning for Togno.

The inspector belonged in a class of his own, definitely one of the worst of his kind. And he could cause trouble. But I'd dealt with even tougher and more dangerous colleagues of his, and I'd gotten off scot-free.

Campagna didn't give up until we lowered the metal roller blinds. He'd spent a shitty day hunting someone he hadn't been able to find and for all I knew a long time might go by before he'd get a chance to talk to him.

On my way home, strolling down the deserted porticoes, I realized that I'd slipped into a state of euphoric excitement. Buratti, Campagna, the fat man in the hospital, Togno, and Signora Palazzolo. The machinery entwined their various fates, and the one turning the handle was always me. I noticed with satisfaction the development of a pretty substantial erection. I turned a loving thought to Martina, I was going to give her the pleasure that she deserved. Gemma, on the other hand, was in the doghouse. She'd be left to watch, struggling to digest the tripe that I'd made her eat for dinner, too.

CHAPTER ELEVEN

Who was that?" Beniamino asked when I hung up the phone.

"Campagna."

He couldn't conceal a grimace of disappointment. "Any news?"

"Togno has vanished," I replied. "But the cop did have something interesting to tell me, which is that his wife, a certain Maria José Pagliaro, used to be a high-end prostitute. He questioned her and she clammed up, but his gut tells him that she knows a lot more than she's saying."

"And he wants you to go get to know her."

"Right. He gave me the address."

Beniamino, sitting on the expensive sofa in the lovers' apartment, slowly lit a cigarette. He closed his eyes as he took the first drag. "You guys got yourselves involved in a dangerous game," he said. "The cops play by their own rules, and those rules are always different from ours. This kind of alliance is always a losing bet."

I disagreed. "Without him, we wouldn't have found out much of anything."

"It's my fault, Marco. My fault and no one else's," he blurted out suddenly.

"That's not true."

He jerked to his feet, grabbed my hand, and gripped it hard.

"I should have been here with you guys, my closest friends,

but instead I abandoned you, I couldn't even find the strength to pick up the phone to hear your voices."

"Why not?"

"Because you were there when Sylvie jumped out the window," he replied in a voice so low that I had could barely hear it. "Every time I relive that scene, you guys are there, and I thought that having you around would drive me crazy."

"Then you did the right thing by keeping us at a distance," I replied, totally honestly. "Sylvie's suicide is a wound that will never heal. The sound of her body hitting the pavement tortures me, I feel a pain so intense it's almost physical."

"It was a mistake for me to think that all this suffering affected only me," he confessed. "I did my best to fight my despair by throwing myself into one robbery after another, just hoping I'd find myself in the middle of a firefight. Only my duty to protect Luc and Christine kept me from starting down the road of no return."

"And now?" I asked, fearing the answer.

"I've come back to settle accounts and to stay. For good," he whispered. "When I heard that Max had been wounded I suddenly came to my senses, I opened my eyes and found myself on the brink of a cliff, an instant before tumbling into the void. The fat man saved my life."

"He saved mine too. He shielded me with his body."

"It won't happen again. I swear it."

I wrapped my arms around him to keep from crying. He hugged me hard. Then he went into the kitchen. I heard him rummaging around with the coffeemaker.

I went into the restroom to splash some water on my face. Now that Rossini was here I felt a little calmer. Max's condition was improving and now Christine, playing the role of the fat man's courteous and likeable French girlfriend, was there to look after him. No one would ever have supposed that in her purse she carried a high caliber pistol and that she would have used it without a second's hesitation to protect Max, should the unsuccessful hit man get any unfortunate ideas about coming back to finish the job.

The woman from Marseille had appeared unexpectedly in the surgical wing and had played her part very believably. When she showed up, I'd been sitting in the waiting room, surrounded by the relatives of the other patients. Christine hadn't so much as glanced at me and I was astonished not to see Beniamino with her. I ran into him a few minutes later in a long corridor; he was slipping coins into a vending machine that dispensed hot drinks.

"I need a cup of coffee," was the way he said hello. "I drove all night long. I was in Brittany when our friend called. I went by to pick her up and now here we are."

"*Ciao,* Beniamino."

He'd looked at me with clear, tired eyes. "*Ciao*, Marco."

"We're in trouble," I'd told him. "We need help."

"The people who need to pay are going to pay."

I had brought him up to speed on everything that had happened while I drove him back to the apartment that Signora Oriana Pozzi Vitali had put at our disposal. The old bandit had listened in silence.

"I know people like Pellegrini all too well," he had commented flatly. "They need to surround themselves with victims so they can experience that constant sense of power that keeps them alive. They are well organized, astute, intelligent predators."

I got the point of what he was saying, but Max and I had made a promise to our client.

"We have to find out the truth," I emphasized. "We can't leave that poor woman moldering in her misery for the rest of her life."

He'd stood up and walked over to me. "I agree. This whole mess is dripping with such cruelty that before we can mete out justice and settle accounts, we need to think of the victims. But I'm not just talking about the Swiss woman or the professor's family. Pellegrini is feeding on a daily basis on the suffering of Gemma and Martina."

"Are you sure?"

"Yes. As I told you, I've had plenty of opportunities to interact with people like this. They're all the same, Mother Nature shaped them all with the same mold, and there's only one way to stop them, and that's to put them six feet under."

"I'm afraid he's not going to be the only one who'll meet that end."

"We're going to have to move very carefully," Rossini had concluded. "But no one will go unpunished."

The next morning we rang the buzzer at Vico dell'Angelo, 34, where Signore and Signora Togno resided. We immediately realized that someone was looking at us through the peephole, and we decided to encourage them to open the door by using the "What, don't you understand that we're cops?" method of knocking, which involves a steady pounding and a string of angry obscenities.

It worked. The door swung open and we found ourselves face to face with a woman who looked about thirty-five, frightened and angry. Dark haired, well built and lithe. A pretty face, with soft features. Under other circumstances, I'd have tried to flirt with her.

"What kind of manners do you have?" she asked, stepping aside to let us in.

"Somebody from your department already came by yesterday," she told us, clearly referring to Campagna. "And I have to say he behaved like a complete jerk."

"The inspector is a rather peculiar individual," I commented. "But let me assure you that we are very different from him."

Beniamino refused to back me up in my little game. "Because, among other things, we're not from the same department at all," he specified, his tone cutting. "We've never liked cops."

The woman blanched and slumped onto a taupe-gray armchair that clashed with the rest of the furnishings.

"Tell him that there's no need for this," she stammered in terror. "I know how to behave. I didn't tell that cop a thing because I don't know a thing. Federico phoned to say that he'd be away from home for a few days and not to worry. I understand that something's going on, but trust me: there's no need for this."

"There's no need for what, Signora?" I asked.

"Would you stop calling me Signora," she shouted in exasperation. "I know what you're here to do to me, but I told you, there's no need. And he knows that I've always been a good girl. I don't understand why he sent you."

"Why *who* sent us, Signora?" I insisted.

"You really want to have some fun with me, don't you?" she snapped. She was desperately looking for a way out. "Let me talk to him, I'm begging you."

Rossini grabbed a chair and placed it before her. The woman recoiled, afraid he was about to hit her. "We call you 'Signora' because we consider you just that, a lady. We don't care what you've done to make a living," he began to explain calmly, looking her in the eye. "We aren't cops, but we aren't working for Pellegrini either. We only came here to ask you a few questions. Maybe we can help each other out."

"Well then, what do you want?"

It was my turn to talk. "Giorgio Pellegrini. We want him and we want his accomplices."

She was disappointed and she sneered obscenely to make that fact clear. "Get out of here," she told us, jerking her thumb at the door. "You don't know Giorgio. He's untouchable, and you know why? Because he's the fiercest man on the face of the Earth. If you dare stand up to him he'll cut you to pieces, and after he's done with you, it'll be my turn next."

We weren't going to get anywhere like this. She was clearly terrified of Pellegrini. I tried another approach. "You're very well-spoken, I'm guessing you've been to school, right?"

"The *liceo classico*, graduated with the highest possible grades. But then, instead of going on to university like my father wanted me to, I came north and got mixed up with a bad crowd," she explained. "But I know you didn't come down here to listen to the sob story of Maria José Pagliaro, a Sicilian girl with great expectations who ended up in the worst of all worlds, did you?"

"We're interested in hearing anything you're willing to tell us," I replied. "But before you say anything else, I want to tell you the story of two people who were very much in love. Her name is Oriana and his name was Guido."

I showed her the picture of the professor. "He taught at the university. Does that interest you?"

She nodded and stretched out her legs. She was starting to relax. A very good sign. I started talking, leaving out details as needed to protect those involved and our investigation. I took about ten minutes to tell the story because her interest seemed genuine, and I included the part that concerned the woman's husband, La Nena and its proprietor, and Max being shot.

"Federico didn't shoot him," she told us immediately. "At that time of night we were in another club to collect some money owed to Giorgio. A horrible night out."

She immediately noticed the disappointment on our faces. "You'll have to look elsewhere, I'm sorry to tell you."

She pointed to a tray that held bottles and glasses. "Even though it's only eleven in the morning, a lady can still have herself a little drink, can't she?"

I hurried to pour out a little cognac into the appropriate glass. She took a few sips while watching us. "You might not have planned to do it, but you've forced me to come over to your side."

"I don't understand," Beniamino said in surprise.

"If my husband ever found out that you'd been here, Giorgio would know it an instant later, and he'd force me to tell him every single word you said to me. In the end, I'd wind up dead in a dumpster."

"Even if you haven't done anything wrong?" I asked.

"That's his method," she replied, cold as marble. "You really don't know anything about him."

"All we know is it's our job to rid humanity of his existence," Rossini replied.

"That won't be enough. Now I'm going to tell you a story: there were seven of us girls. Six foreigners and me, the only Italian, because there were customers who wanted only certified domestic pussy. We all lived together in a pretty little house on the outskirts of town. We were managed by a woman named Nicoletta, and she reported directly and exclusively to Pellegrini. One day something went wrong and he had to get his affairs in order. The foreign girls all vanished. A week later, so did Nicoletta."

Beniamino and I exchanged a glance. Maria José was confirming the rumors about Pellegrini's involvement in the trafficking of prostitutes with the Maltese mafia.

"I lived in fear," the woman went on. "I was sure I was about to be murdered. I got down on my knees, told him I was willing to do anything, and Giorgio decided to show mercy. He married me off to Federico Togno, telling me to keep an eye on everything he did and report back, to push Federico to do whatever Giorgio wanted. He's turned me into a slave who can never say no. You have no idea of what it means to satisfy every desire of a troll like my husband.

"So now do you understand why I have no intention of facing him after the two of you go out that door? What do you have to offer me? Before you answer, let me warn you: I'd sooner kill myself than go on being a whore. First I was Pellegrini's whore, then I was Federico Togno's. I've had enough."

"You want a new life," I replied.

"Enough money to start over," Beniamino added. "A job and a safe place to live. Far away from here."

"Where?"

"A hotel on the coast of Portugal. I have a friend who just bought the place, and I know that he'd be glad to hire an attractive person who speaks Italian."

"I've been living a shitty life for all these years and just when I'm about to give up you appear out of the blue and offer to rescue me," she murmured under her breath as she started to tremble. "It's not like you're filling my head with pretty words, and then you're just going to kill me, is it?"

Too much emotional uproar for a warm morning in late September. I smiled at her. "You're going to have to trust us. Anyway, you said it yourself: you don't have any other options."

"What do you want to know?"

"Right now you just need to pack your bags," said Rossini. "We'll have plenty of time to talk at lunch."

Maria José knew enough to give us an exhaustive overview of Pellegrini's criminal pursuits. She had pieced it all together from conversations among her customers, many of them tied to the network of corruption organized by Sante Brianese, and also thanks to her husband's confidences. His boss maneuvered him from La Nena like a puppet on a string, and he'd even pushed him to commit murder.

We were still a long way away from solving the case of Professor Di Lello's murder, but we were finally on the right path.

While Maria José was resting in Christine's bedroom, and while Christine was in the hospital looking after Max, Rossini organized her escape. An old smuggler from Punta Sabbioni who Rossini trusted would come and pick her up at dawn the next day. A powerful speedboat would set off for the Croatian coast where another smuggler would take her to Zagreb airport. It would be hard even for the cops to retrace her route and, most importantly, it would take them a long time to identify her final destination. It all depended on what became of her husband. Right then, I was ready to bet that his future as a paid henchman was no longer all that bright.

The woman from Marseille came back a little after seven that evening. She was tired. She had time for a shower, and then she'd be back at the fat man's bedside. But Beniamino had other plans.

"Get yourself dolled up, I'm taking you out to dinner," he announced. "Tonight Marco will be taking your place."

It struck me as a perfect way to take her mind off things until I asked: "So where are you planning to go eat?"

"La Nena," he replied, unable to restrain a wicked smile. "I made a reservation for 9:30."

"Are you sure that's a good idea?" I asked, even though I already knew the answer.

"Certainly," he replied indignantly. "We're going to show up on his doorstep to make it clear that this is a declaration of war, which will give him a chance to choose how to react. It's the least we can do."

I was tempted to remind him that this very approach had prolonged a gang war that had ruined our lives, but I bit my tongue, opting instead for a useless appeal to common sense. "Giorgio Pellegrini belongs to a different generation, certain niceties are beyond his understanding, and what's more, he'll only take advantage. You're giving him a head start."

The old bandit threw both arms wide. "Even if he is a piece of shit, I don't intend to stop behaving properly."

"But why Christine, then?" I blurted out. "I'm the one who ought to be going."

He waved his finger. "No. I want Pellegrini to meet a 'dangerous' woman, someone who could gladly send him into the heareafter without batting an eyelash, just for the pleasure of doing a little housecleaning."

I surrendered and went off to drink a small glass of Calvados. At least, that had been my intention, though I couldn't resist and poured myself a double.

When I got to the hospital I followed Christine's instructions. Sure enough, she had already softened up the medical personnel not only with tips, but with her own winning personality. Before I knew it, I was sitting by Max's bedside.

"You're growing a mustache," he noticed immediately. "It doesn't even look all that bad."

His voice was so labored as to be unrecognizable and overall, he looked like shit.

"You don't look all that bad either," I retorted with a smile.

"They told me I'd have to change my lifestyle, and in the meantime they've put me on a diet."

"So I heard."

"Can you just picture me counting calories?"

"I've got a pretty good imagination."

"The other day I opened my eyes and sitting by the bed was a beautiful woman looking at me," he told me, with a trace of a smile. "It was the psychologist. She told me I wouldn't make it on my own."

I laid a hand on his chest. An unusual thing to do. My dad used to do it when he came in to tell me goodnight. "You saved my life, Max."

"I didn't mean to," he said evasively.

I brought him up-to-date on everything that had happened since the minute he'd been shot.

"We're getting closer to settling accounts," my partner commented.

"That's what Beniamino wants, but he'll have to wait to pull out the guns until we have a complete profile of the gang of lovers," I explained. "We can't run the risk of one of these bastards getting away and starting up again somewhere else."

"It was Pellegrini's idea, there's no doubt about it. That guy is a teeming sewer of twisted but brilliant projects."

I had a hard time finding a parking place near the apartment and found myself walking past the place where we'd been ambushed. For the past few days I'd avoided the location, and now I stopped to study the details. I realized that I was still upset. And yet I'd been through far worse.

Maria José was watching TV in the living room. She was dressed to the nines, and the two wheeled suitcases she'd stuffed with everything she was unwilling to leave behind were close at hand.

"It'll be another couple of hours before they come pick you up," I told her as I poured myself a drink.

"Time's passing so slowly tonight," she said, flashing me an uneasy smile.

"You're telling me," I shot back as I sat down next to her.

We sat wordlessly watching an episode of a popular American show in which detectives seek the truth through the lenses of a microscope or in the color of chemical reagents. Lucky stiffs.

Often, I glanced over at our guest out of the corner of my eye. There were unmistakable signs of weariness and tension on her face. She was escaping the horror into which despicable men had forced her, by taking a leap into the void.

CHAPTER TWELVE

Ten minutes to closing time and those two still hadn't asked for the check. I'd recognized Rossini immediately. I'd happened to see his picture in the papers once or twice, but I would have figured it out anyway just from his style. A slightly out-of-fashion double-breasted suit, a regimental tie with a Windsor knot, wrapped eight full turns to get it just right, handmade shoes. The outfit of a topflight gangster. As I walked past their table he "just happened" to stretch out his arm, and his cuff pulled back to reveal his bracelets. Until that moment I'd been certain that it was nothing but a legend, but he himself had chosen to show off his collection of scalps. Each bracelet was a dead man. Poor old asshole, I'd definitely killed more than he had.

The woman wasn't much to look at. Her features were coarse, as was the French that she spoke, no refinement at all in her clothing. Still, she had the body, the posture, and the alert gaze of someone who was accustomed to action. She wouldn't be any use to me because that kind of woman doesn't bring in cash. I'd have to kill her, just as I'd kill her date, but I'd definitely make sure I thoroughly enjoyed her company, in every way imaginable, just to break her spirit before she died. She reminded me of a Spanish woman I'd organized an armed robbery with once. She was so troublesome that in the end I'd had to sell her to two Croatian war criminals just to get rid of her.

I'd taken care not to say hello to Rossini and his girlfriend or treat them as respected guests. I'd sent them my least experienced waiter but they hadn't batted an eye. I'd watched them closely the whole time. They'd played the part of a happy couple enjoying their night out, tasting specialties and sampling wines as if money were no object, but discreetly, so as not to attract attention.

Now they were nursing a couple of glasses of grappa and talking quietly. The only sound you could hear in the restaurant was the waiters cleaning up and preparing the tables for the next day.

I checked the time. Just six minutes left. I wrote up the check and took it over to them personally.

"The restaurant is about to close," I announced.

"We're not worried about that. I'm sure it will open again under new management," said Rossini.

I burst out laughing. That holdover from a bygone era really was funny. He'd come to announce to me that he planned to take me out. And in my own restaurant, no less.

"I appreciate the kind words," I retorted. "But don't think I return the sentiment."

"I never doubted that would be the case," Rossini replied solicitously. "We have nothing in common."

I decided to push a few buttons. "Not necessarily. I might have a few ideas about your guest," I said in French.

The woman was quick to reply. "If you only knew the ideas I've had about you."

A dangerous whore. One I'd have to put down without a second thought. "Well, see you again soon," I said, pointing them to the door.

Rossini took a quick look at the check, pulled out a few banknotes and tossed them on the table. "Sleep on that thought," he suggested with a cordial smile.

I watched them as they walked off arm in arm, chatting cheerfully. Rossini was too sure of himself. Something must have happened that made him think he could come challenge me with that night's ultimatum.

At last the time came to lock the door and lower the metal roller blinds. After making sure I wasn't being followed, even though I was certain the old man played fair, I headed for the Centra brothers' house.

I waited a good fifteen minutes, observing the street, the closed windows, the parked cars. I didn't spot anything alarming and so I announced my arrival on my cell phone. Togno opened the door. He was irritated.

"Where the hell did you send me?" he burst out as he led the way to the old workshop. "These two are out of their minds. Where did you find them?"

"Everything all right?" I asked, cutting him off. Togno was complaining too much for a foot soldier.

"It was perfectly pointless to bring that poor woman here. Her sweetheart is willing to do anything to get her back safe and sound. It would have been enough just to demand money," he commented.

"That's the kind of judgment call that I'll make on my own."

Federico immediately changed his attitude. "I'd never dream of criticizing you and you know it, it's just that I can't wait to get out of this place."

"How far along are the negotiations?"

"Tomorrow morning Rosario Panichi is going to the bank to empty out a safe deposit box. What with jewelry and cash, there's at least three hundred thousand euros in there."

"I'll let you know when to call him, all right?"

He looked at me, surprised. "Maybe I didn't make myself clear, but tomorrow afternoon we can wrap up the deal."

I gave him a slap on the cheek, just a little harder than necessary. "I wonder if you understand that I just told you to call him only when I say so?" I asked, enunciating my words clearly.

Togno fell silent. The closer we got to the cellar workshop, the clearer we could hear Furio and Toni's cackling laughter.

I stopped in a dark corner of the stairs that offered a complete view of the area below. The Centra brothers were playing a card game of *briscola* with the hostage, enjoying themselves like a couple of kids. The woman was dressed in a white slip stained with red wine. She could barely hold the cards in her hands. She was alternating between tears and laughter.

"What have they done to her?"

"Every time she loses they make her drink another glass," he explained in a low voice. "She's already drunk and if you ask me before long they're going to screw her."

"See if you can keep that from happening."

"Not on your life. They're animals. I wouldn't put it past them to take it out on me and personally I value my virgin ass."

"All right. I've seen enough," I said, retracing my steps.

My henchman snickered. "Leaving so soon? Don't you want to say hello to the two kid brothers?"

"Signora Palazzolo knows me. She always used to come to La Nena," I replied coldly. And then I snapped. "Would you tell me what the fuck is wrong with you? You've been complaining, you've been overstepping some bounds. I'm your boss and I've given you a job worth fifty thousand euros. You need to show me some respect."

"You're right, I apologize yet again," he mumbled. "It's just that I don't know what's become of Maria José. There's no answer on either the home phone or her cell . . ."

"And why would you be making calls to your little wifey-poo while you're running a kidnapping?" I asked him furiously.

It dawned on Federico that he'd fucked up again and he hastened to explain. "Maria José was supposed to lay a bet on a horse race. Since I couldn't do it, I wanted to tell her to go see Longoni herself."

Sergio Longoni. A courier for a network of illegal bookies. He used to spend time at La Nena until I made it clear to him he needed to clear out. "I don't like the way you're acting,

Federico," I told him. "You're reckless, you take pointless risks, and you're putting us all in danger."

"Oh, don't exaggerate, Giorgio. You can't really consider this to be a real kidnapping. These two will never report us to the police. They'll keep quiet."

I had no interest in wasting time teaching the basics to a brainless vegetable like Federico Togno.

"Maria José might have gone to stay with some girlfriend, or a relative. She just took a little time off," I hypothesized, just to see what he'd say.

He shook his head grimly. "She knows that if she's not always available, I'll beat her black and blue," he hissed. "Otherwise you tell me what the fuck the point of keeping her like a lady is if she's not always available?"

"Maybe she's pissed off at you and she's holding a grudge."

"No. She probably got run over by a car or something, or she's going to wish she had because the minute I lay my hands on her I'll beat her like a drum. She made me miss out on a sure thing."

A sudden intuition. A premonition. I held out my hand. "House keys," I ordered.

"The keys to *my* house?"

I was barely able to restrain my anger. "I already have the keys to mine in my pocket, Federico!"

"What do you need them for?"

"I'm going to take a look around," I replied. "I'm doing you a favor. Instead of going to get some sleep after a hard day's work, I'm going to make sure that nothing's happened to your wife."

He pulled out a key ring and dropped it into the palm of my hand. "Thank you, Giorgio."

The apartment was immersed in darkness. I switched on the light in the front hall and announced myself so that I wouldn't be attacked by a hysterical, frightened woman. I noticed immediately that something was wrong. Drawers pulled open, things scattered across the floor. When I got to the bedroom I was sure of it: Maria José had hastily put all her things into a suitcase and fled.

I went into the kitchen and looked in the refrigerator for something refreshing. Dry mouth, a collateral effect of being ripped off. I had to settle for a bottle of white wine.

As I was uncorking it I wondered just what I'd ever seen in a 500-euro-a-trick hooker like Maria José Pagliaro, what had convinced me she was so special that I chose not to sell her off with the others. I would have gotten good money for her, too. Instead I'd decided it was a good idea to keep her and marry her off to Federico Togno, my disappointing flunky. I'd fooled myself into thinking that I'd created the perfect couple, forever dedicated to satisfying my every wish.

A dramatic mistake. Possibly a fatal one. The only time I'd forgotten the principle that says the superfluous should always be eliminated, and fate was already presenting me with the bill.

Rossini and Buratti were certainly behind that whore's disappearance. They'd shown up and she'd cut a deal with them. She didn't know anything about the most important operations, but she knew about the old prostitution ring and everything concerning Togno.

Put that together with the other information they must have assembled and now they had a pretty complete picture of the situation. They knew that I was behind the professor's disappearance and Rossini had felt obliged to come throw down the gauntlet.

There was no way to settle this matter without paying at least a part of the bill, but I was going to shove that gauntlet up his ass. They too were making a fatal error by underestimating me.

I washed the glass and wiped my fingerprints before leaving. And I took great care not to warn that pathetic cuckold Federico. I had more important things to do.

I went back into town, parked the car, and walked to an old apartment building I had the keys to. I opened the front door and walked downstairs to the basement garages. The one I owned was number 7. It was registered as belonging to an elderly aunt of Gemma's who of course had no idea she owned it. It contained some old furniture. A credenza held a bag with money, jewelry, weapons, and IDs, everything I'd need to go on the run for a good long time. And get a chance to start over. I checked everything twice. I could no longer afford the luxury of a mistake.

I got home around seven in the morning. Martina and Gemma were still fully dressed, awaiting my orders for the night. They were confused, worried, and afraid to ask for explanations. I pointed at Gemma. "Call your friend Buratti and tell him that I'll expect him and Rossini at La Nena after it closes. Got it?"

The two women nodded like a couple of marionettes. "Pack your bags for a week's vacation, I want you out of here by noon."

"But this morning I have my pilates class, and a massage too," my wife replied.

"Shut up!" her girlfriend ordered her, then asked me: "Where should we go?"

I shrugged. "Wherever you want. I don't care," I replied. "I want this house empty by no later than noon."

Gemma shot to her feet. She'd understood the gravity of the situation. For the first time I hadn't given them a specific order and the alarm bells going off in her head must have been deafening.

She took my hand. "Giorgio, please," she stammered.

I jerked my hand away and locked myself in my bedroom. I was sleepy and right then all I wanted was some shut-eye. I needed to be fit and rested if I wanted to put Plan B into motion. Salvage whatever can be saved, screw the enemy.

CHAPTER THIRTEEN

This is Gemma."

"I recognized your number," I replied, realizing that it was 7:30 in the morning.

"I need to talk to you."

"Are you doing this on his orders?" I asked. By now there was no point in pretending any longer.

"I have a message from Giorgio," she replied. "I could tell you over the phone but I don't understand what's happening and doubtless you know more than I do."

"Fine. But I name the place."

"You don't trust me," Gemma stated bitterly.

"No, I don't."

For a few seconds she said nothing. "Well, where then?"

In situations like this one I always chose bars in shopping centers. I knew one in Vicenza, just outside the toll barrier on the autostrada, which also happened to afford the protection of a fair number of armed security guards.

"At eleven o'clock," I said.

I went into the bathroom to freshen up after a night in the hospital with Max and, while I was there, took a look in the mirror to see how my mustache was coming along. The problem is that once the hair starts coming in, you have to choose a style, and I just wasn't ready. I needed a woman to give me proper advice. Maybe I could ask Gemma, even if she didn't seem to be in the right mood. Pellegrini had made her a messenger, and that could only mean he had a clear plan in mind. By now, there were no doubts about the inevitability of a fight, and as far as I was concerned, that came as a relief. The risk of winding up murdered or in prison serving hard time was a constant source of concern, but the whole story and its protagonist, Giorgio Pellegrini, were so atrociously tawdry and cruel that we needed to put an end to it, and urgently. That was what was right, and what was necessary.

In the kitchen I found Beniamino and Christine having breakfast. The old bandit was wearing a pair of his legendary silk pajamas. The woman from Marseille wore only a white T-shirt that barely covered her bottom. Both of them were eagerly sipping from cups of espresso and milk, and dipping long, hard, sweet biscuits in their cups. I hadn't seen those biscuits since I was a boy.

I made do with a cup of coffee while I briefed them on my conversation with Gemma.

"Do you think this is an ambush of some kind?" Rossini asked.

"No," I replied. "Pellegrini has something in mind, but if I know his type I think it's something more refined."

"I think so too," said my friend. "So you'll go alone. I have to get my hands on some equipment. Christine'll keep an eye on Max."

"Do you really think he's in danger or is this just a standard precaution?" I asked dubiously. "One more gun might be useful, since we don't know how many men Pellegrini might have."

"Max is our weak point," he explained. "Handsome Giorgio respects no rules and is perfectly capable of stooping low enough to kill a wounded man, knowing the effect that it would have on us."

I shuddered. "I don't even want to think about it," I whispered. Then I turned to Christine: "Say, why isn't Luc around?"

Christine shot Rossini a look. They exchanged a brief glance and then both burst out laughing. "My husband's laid up in bed with a gunshot wound, too," she confessed, amidst the laughter. "He caught a blast of shotgun pellets in the seat of his pants from a farmer who caught him stealing a chicken from his henhouse."

"I don't believe it."

"I married a chicken thief," she added, laughing so hard that tears came to her eyes.

Rossini too was laughing unrestrainedly. Soon I joined in. What a jerk, that Luc, shot in the ass like a rank beginner.

I got there a little ahead of time, parked my Felicia, and took a look around the shopping center, idly window-shopping. Some of the shops were closed, others announced they would soon be under new management. An embarrassment of sales and special offers. Even the wealthy city of Vicenza was showing signs of the financial crisis in a temple of urban consumption. I stopped to buy a pack of cigarettes. The tobacconist asked if I cared to try my luck with any of the countless scratch & win lottery cards wallpapering the shop. I thanked him, knowing that there were thousands of counterfeit scratch & win cards in circulation. I was tempted to tell him so, but there were other customers in the shop. The one standing right behind me tapped me on the shoulder. "If you had bought one, which one would you have chosen? Sorry to bother you, but luck has been turning her nose up at me for a while, and I was thinking you might be on her good side."

I pointed to one and slipped out of the store with a sigh of relief. Being lucky at gambling is something that comes to only a select few. I knew one or two and, naturally, they were women.

Gemma came in, holding Martina's hand. When I sat down at their table I realized that Pellegrini's wife was shaken, confused.

"I can't see when I'm going to make up for the activities I missed this morning," she said, as soon as she saw me. "There's no way to fit them into the coming days."

Her girlfriend was stroking her hand. "Don't worry about it. I'll take care of it. Here, have something to drink."

I stared at Gemma. Her hair was a mess, she didn't have a speck of makeup on. "What's going on?" I asked.

"Giorgio sent us on vacation," she replied. "For a week."

"A vacation means cancelling the activities," Martina pointed out. "The problem is the ones from this morning."

I couldn't believe my ears. "So Giorgio has decided that you needed a little time off, and you jump to obey."

"Giorgio decides everything," Gemma replied, exaggeratedly resolute. "And we're fine with it."

"Are you really sure of that?" I asked.

"I always have been."

I took a sip of spritz and changed the subject. "On the phone you said you had a message from Pellegrini."

"He'll see you tonight at La Nena, after closing time."

"A tempting invitation," I commented ironically.

"Will you go?"

"I don't know," I replied. "And either way, I'm certainly not going to tell you."

She nodded, then she turned to her friend. "Go do some shopping, Martina," she said, pulling a wad of cash out of the pocket of her rumpled skirt suit.

The other woman didn't have to be told twice and leapt to her feet. "I was just starting to get tired of your complicated conversation," she muttered. "It's all because of your diet. Too many toxins in your liver tend to undermine your ability to think clearly."

Gemma waited for Martina to be out of earshot before asking a question that caught me off guard. "Who's going to win?"

"We are," I replied confidently. "The era of handsome Giorgio is coming to an end. A matter of days, if not hours."

She bit her lip. "Until this morning I was positive, absolutely positive that it was the other way round," she explained. "Then I saw a hint of uncertainty in his eyes. That had never happened before."

I shrugged. "I have no idea what he's planning but I can guarantee that his fate is sealed."

"What about us?"

"Are you serious?" I hissed, aghast. "This is your chance to finally free yourselves of your 'lord and master' and start a new life. You should leap at the chance."

"You don't understand . . ."

"No. You're the one who doesn't understand," I interrupted her. "Martina is slipping dangerously into mental illness and you're willingly hurling yourself into an abyss. I don't know anything about you and your past but one thing is certain. Your 'King of Hearts,' Giorgio Pellegrini, isn't the treatment, he's the disease, the virus that's devouring you."

Her eyes welled up with tears. "Will he die?"

I decided to tell her the truth. That woman had a right to know in spite of her indestructible loyalty to that sack of garbage. "Probably. I hope so with every ounce of strength in my body. He's hurt too many people."

"You don't seem strong enough to beat him," she objected. "Maybe you're overestimating yourself."

"My friend will take care of him."

"Who? The fat man in the hospital?"

"No. Someone else."

"You sure have a lot of friends."

"You don't," I retorted, cruelly. "You've been forced to serve as a lady's companion to a loony just to keep loneliness at bay."

"And to be Giorgio's whore," she added, carefully enunciating her words. "You have no idea how good I am at keeping him happy."

There was a strain of despair in her voice that left me speechless. Gemma stood up and walked away wearily. I wished her good luck.

"He actually wants a meeting with us in his restaurant?"

Beniamino asked in surprise a couple of hours later. He had come back from Punta Sabbioni with a duffel bag full of weapons and ammunition. A sawed off pump-action shotgun, and a couple of handguns with silencers that he was now cleaning and oiling.

"That's right," I replied, giving the arsenal a worried glance. I'd never much liked weapons and I'd never been willing to pick one up. Not even to learn how to shoot. There was a very simple reason: I'd never have been able to carry the weight of a dead man on my conscience. I'd always been clear on this point and I left it up to Rossini to manage violence in all its various declensions, because he—unlike me—believed it was a necessity, when justice demanded it.

Max, too, was careful to steer clear of weapons, but that was for different reasons, to do more with his physical condition. He was too much of a butterfingers to be sure that a gun in his hand wasn't a one-way ticket to suicide, or at best to shooting himself in the foot.

"All right then," the old bandit cut the conversation short as he peered down the barrel of a gun.

It wasn't all right with me. "I don't see why we should walk voluntarily into a trap. I don't believe he's inviting us there to offer us a nightcap."

"We can't refuse the invitation," Rossini shot back. "I went into Pellegrini's place and challenged him. Now he's calling us back to clarify his position. At the first hint of a threat I'll kill him and anyone else who tries to put anything over on us."

I heaved an exasperated sigh. "Do you think that Pellegrini doesn't know that you're going to show up armed?"

"I'm sure he's anticipated every move."

"In that case, why go?"

"Because we're the ones who started down this path and now we need to stick with it until we reach the end," he snorted, annoyed. "All this chatter is messing up my concentration and these guns need my full and undivided attention."

"Otherwise they might take offense," I joked as I lit a cigarette.

"That's exactly right. Especially the .45s. If you don't treat them like ladies, they'll pay you back just when you need them most."

"Cut it out, Beniamino. You seem a little crazy when you talk like that."

"Well then, let me work in peace while I enjoy this moment of lunacy," he snickered.

He shot me a wink. It was his way of telling me I could rely on him.

The last customers straggled out of La Nena a little after midnight. They walked past us complaining about the prices and surprised at the proprietor's arrogance. Pellegrini was on edge, and he was taking it out on his customers. Maybe he wasn't so sure that his plan was going to work.

We decided to go in when the staff was still there, trusting that that would be one more line of defense against an ambush. Handsome Giorgio didn't so much as blink. He loudly thanked us for coming in and invited us to follow him into a small dining room where a waiter brought a bottle of champagne and three flutes. He filled one glass and drained it in a single gulp.

"You'd never have agreed to drink with me, so I spared you the awkwardness," he justified his rudeness. "And after all, this fine French bubbly only helps to set the right, old-fashioned tone. The two self-respecting criminals who drop by to settle accounts with the bad guy du jour. What do you two call each other when you're alone? Pepé? Jojo?"

I exchanged a glance with Beniamino. This asshole was trying to rile us up, but we'd come just to hear what he had to say, so we sat in silence.

He stuck his forefinger right at me. "You scared Gemma. You told her my time was running out."

"The simple truth, then," Rossini broke in, pulling out a pistol and laying it on the table in accordance with time-honored ritual. "Your filthy career is coming to an end."

Pellegrini pretended to shudder. "Why, what a terrible fright! I almost had a heart attack."

Something wasn't right. He clearly had an ace up his sleeve.

"What are you going to do, shoot me here, you pathetic old retired crook?" handsome Giorgio mocked him, laughing in his face.

"No, though I'll admit I'm strongly tempted," Rossini replied calmly. "But the time will come, and when it does it will be a pleasure."

"You're just a couple of losers," he went on insulting us. "You're nobodies, coming in here to try to meddle in my business."

"You're through, Pellegrini," I blurted. "End the charade and tell us about Guido Di Lello. How did he die?"

I was sure he'd try to deny everything, but instead he had no trouble admitting his involvement. "It's the Swiss woman who's paying you, right?"

"Yes."

"Does she just want the truth or does she want to make sure that whoever took her lover away pays the price?"

"That's none of your business," I replied.

The proprietor of La Nena was enjoying himself. He seemed annoyed, offended perhaps, but not scared in the slightest.

"I understand: she didn't hire you to avenge the memory of that idiot professor of hers," he said. "In that case, turn me over to the cops. Now."

"We have no intention of involving the police," Beniamino said evenly.

Pellegrini feigned surprise. "Oh, no? And yet for some reason you're thick as thieves with Padua police HQ, since the news of the clandestine background checks on Buratti and Max the Memory carried out by that cuckolded idiot Federico Togno leaked from the offices of the Mobile Squad."

He was referring to Inspector Campagna but there was no point in pursuing that line of conversation. Useless and dangerous to provide him with any information.

"You've no doubt noticed that I just described Togno as a cuckolded idiot," Giorgio went on. "And I didn't choose the term at random, since you took his wife away from him."

"She gave us plenty of useful information," Rossini said. "The details that we needed to fill in the big picture."

Pellegrini threw out both arms. "I admit my misjudgment. I underestimated the potential downside of a second-rate whore."

He suddenly grabbed his cell phone and slammed it down on the table. "Call your trusted cops or else walk out that door and never show your faces around here again."

I sighed. "We've delved into your past," I started telling him. "We know that you've been in the service of powerful men like Sante Brianese and that you've always been ready and willing to sell out whoever you had to in order to keep from paying for your crimes.

"You're challenging us to call the law on you because, no doubt, you're in a position to negotiate and you'd be able to get away scot-free this time too.

"But we've made up our minds to stop you, to shut down your illegal activities, and put an end to the harm you've been doing. Once and for all. I confess that we'd like to know the truth about what became of Guido Di Lello to satisfy the needs of our client, but if we can't do it, we'll be able to live with ourselves. The complete absence of room for bargaining means that we can't force you to talk."

Pellegrini rolled his eyes. "Are the two of you really going to keep to this cut-rate script from a movie from the fifties? Brush off the mothballs and look around you with fresh eyes because, and I say this in total honesty, you're so pathetic that, in the end, you make me feel a little tenderly toward you. If you want, I'd be glad to hire you, so you can entertain our guests with your ridiculous Jean Gabin routine."

"I'm getting tired of your insults," old Rossini said menacingly.

"Do you care to make a bet that you're going to have to go on taking them for a good long time?"

I knew my friend far too well not to know he was starting to reach the end of his rope and that the next insult would be washed off with blood. I stood up.

"Let's go," I said to Beniamino. "The visit ends here, as do the good manners."

Rossini grabbed his pistol and put it away in his shoulder holster without ever taking his eyes off handsome Giorgio, who caught me off guard once again by inviting us to stay a while longer.

"We're still not finished here," he explained. "The reason I asked for this meeting, aside from the priceless pleasure of your lovely company, is to come to an agreement that both parties find reasonable and satisfactory."

"You don't have anything to trade that's valuable enough to save your skin," I shot back sarcastically.

Pellegrini shook his head in disappointment. "Only a dilettante would talk like that," he chided me. "You still have a lot to learn from yours truly."

"We're listening," Rossini snapped brusquely.

"I'll make sure you catch the gang down to every last man. Federico Togno together with the two guys who ran the kidnapping and killed the professor and buried his body, and shot your overweight buddy too. But you in exchange forget you ever even heard of yours truly."

We showed no interest and Beniamino laid out the way we saw things. "You're the boss, the brains, the mastermind. The first name on the list, get it? Or do I have to tell you the story of the serpent's head?"

"We'll round up the others later," I added. "Togno will pop out of the woodwork eventually, and when he does he'll turn over his accomplices."

"Your reasoning is impeccable," Giorgio complimented me, "but I'm certain that you will be willing to accept my offer because right now the gang is up and running. There's a hostage in their hands, still alive right now, but tomorrow who can say . . . and given the fact that your hearts overflow with charitable sentiments, I know that, in order to save that hostage's life, you're going to meet me halfway."

Bastard son of a bitch. He'd made an end run around us. The choice was a simple one because we had no alternatives. The life of the hostage made our desire to bring Pellegrini to justice a secondary concern. I was sincerely impressed with his perverse brilliance as well as the ruthless way he had brought us to this point. He knew from the very beginning that we'd have to accept his terms.

I was pretty sure that Beniamino felt the same way I did and I was surprised when he said: "The truth is, you only need to put in an anonymous phone call to the cops and you could arrange for the hostage to be rescued. But then unfortunately your accomplices would give them your name and you'd wind up in prison."

"And sadly ready and willing to talk about your own involvement," Pellegrini hastened to point out.

"So you want us to save the hostage by killing Togno and those other two," Rossini went on.

"They're guilty of terrible crimes, and according to your chivalrous code, they deserve to die."

"And in exchange you want to be left in peace."

"For the rest of my life."

I objected. "No, you can't get away with it like this," I hissed furiously. "If the hostage returns home, if you tell us the truth about what became of the professor, you can save your skin. But then you're going to have to go far away and abandon restaurant, house, wife, and girlfriend."

"Don't be ridiculous," he replied defiantly. "You're forgetting about the kidnap victim, a poor old woman who's in her early sixties."

"We'll be sorry not to be able to help her, but that'll just mean that the day I kill you will be all the sweeter," Rossini bluffed, shifting his chair.

Beniamino was already turning the door handle when handsome Giorgio said: "Fine. We'll do it your way."

The Centra brothers' house and old workshop were immersed in shadows. No outside lights, shutters fastened tight. Beniamino carefully scrutinized the whole layout, asking Pellegrini the same questions about the floor plan and the location of his men over and over again. Handsome Giorgio, comfortably seated in the back, replied mechanically and without contradicting himself. Meanwhile, I was mulling over every single word we'd exchanged back at the restaurant, trying to figure out all the tricks he'd used to screw us. At a certain point I had the right intuition.

"When was the woman kidnapped?"

"A few days ago," he replied evasively. He'd already sniffed out what I had in mind.

"You miserable piece of shit," I blurted, turning to Rossini. "He ordered his henchmen to kidnap the woman just so he'd have a bargaining chip. He'd sensed we were on his trail and he prepared an escape hatch."

"If I wasn't handcuffed I'd clap my hands in appreciation of your wisdom; if you'd like I can still let out little shouts of jubilation: yay, yay," said Pellegrini, amusing himself once again.

Beniamino shrugged. "It doesn't change a thing. The hostage's life is more important this vicious little troll's. We'll settle up with him some other time."

"In that case, you'd better hurry," Pellegrini challenged him, "because once you reach retirement age it's tough to aim accurately. Your hands start shaking and your eyesight is never the same. A few more years and you'll be needing a nurse."

Rossini didn't react. Handsome Giorgio was having fun with us, certain that he could loll about in safety. We'd hold up our end of the bargain and no one would harm a hair on his head, but what the bastard didn't know or wasn't counting on was that the next time he crossed paths with my friend, he'd be a dead man. His life would be cut short by a shower of lead. That's why the old bandit was putting up with his insults and not reacting. There was definitely going to be a sequel to this story.

"In five minutes, we're going in," Rossini announced.

"Just enough time for you to tell us what happened to Guido Di Lello," I said.

"Happy to," he retorted cheerfully. "In part because I believe that the professor's story will help you understand that the Swiss woman really didn't deserve so much attention after all."

The restaurateur possessed a sick gift of the gab that allowed him to render interesting even a story steeped in needless cruelty.

I felt the need to recap what he'd said, just to be sure I'd understood correctly. "Are you saying that you let two psychopaths slaughter a young university professor and bury his body in an unmarked grave, just so you could punish his wealthy lover for refusing to pay the ransom?"

"Exactly," he said in the voice of a wise elder statesman. "Di Lello was a miserable chump, a coward willing to sell out completely in exchange to save his skin and safeguard his secret."

"Just like you," I broke in. "You've done the same thing all your life, even now you're ready to let three people die as long as your miserable life is spared."

"Why, what language, Buratti!" he said derisively. "So you aren't the amoeba I always took you for. The difference between me and Di Lello is that in his situation I'd have come out alive and stronger than ever for one simple reason: I always land on my feet."

Rossini pulled pack the lever on his pump-action shotgun to load a cartridge filled with pellets normally used to hunt wild boar. A sinister sound that for a brief moment succeeded in wiping the arrogant expression off Pellegrini's face. The man picked up his cell phone and alerted Togno of his imminent arrival.

The flunky's jaw dropped in astonishment when he found himself facing a gun aimed at the center of his chest. He turned to look at his boss who quickly reassured him: "Keep calm, Federico, I've made a deal with these gentlemen."

But Togno wasn't completely stupid. "What kind of a deal could you have made with Buratti?" he asked, pointing at me.

Rossini slipped his hand into his jacket, pulled out the pistol equipped with a silencer, and aimed it at the ex-carabiniere's forehead. "Where are the other two?" he asked in a relaxed voice.

"In the cellar workshop."

The old bandit pulled the trigger and Togno flopped down onto the floor without a sound. For the first time I glimpsed a gleam of admiring concern in the look on handsome Giorgio's face. Now he realized that Rossini was more than just a legend from a bygone age.

"Lead the way," I ordered.

He walked ahead of us with a confident gait, and when we reached the underground room that had once served as a workshop we found ourselves face to face with an absurdist scene, worthy of a pair of brutes like the Centra brothers. The hostage was wearing nothing but a pair of rubber boots that were far too large for her. She was holding a broom and trying to clean the floor while the two kidnappers pelted her with a ridiculous array of objects along with a barrage of laughter and insults.

"That's enough," Rossini barked. "On your knees, with your hands on your heads. You too, Pellegrini."

The three men did as they were told. The owners of the house, in heavy dialect, started peppering their boss with questions. He tried in vain to calm them down. Rossini was forced to intervene, distributing blows with the butt of the rifle.

I took care of the woman. I draped an old blanket over her and accompanied her to a bathroom upstairs. In one room I found her clothing and a purse and I took them to her, telling her she was free to get dressed.

She moved slowly, as if she was having a hard time recovering the ability to do familiar things. I urged her to hurry. She looked up at me. "Are you like them?"

I seized her hand. "No, Signora. We're taking you home."

"Are you from the police?"

"This is a secret operation," I whispered in a voice dripping with complicity. "You can't tell a soul."

She nodded. "Don't worry. I've been keeping secrets all my life."

"I'll be back in a few minutes, but you need to stay right where you are, understood?"

"You're going to kill those two monsters, aren't you?"

I closed the door and went downstairs. Rossini was smoking, his gun trained on the three men.

"Did you question them?" I asked.

"I've seen more than enough," he replied. "How is the woman?"

"She seems tough. In time, she'll recover."

Beniamino stepped over to one of the brothers and placed the muzzle of his gun at the back of his head. "Where's the gun you used to shoot my friend?"

The man pointed to a drawer in a worktable. I opened it and among an assortment of tools I found the .22 caliber pistol that had wounded Max. I handed it to Rossini, who checked the clip. He removed all the bullets but two. Then he told handsome Giorgio to stand up and come closer.

"You can kill these two troglodytes," he told him as he removed his handcuffs. "They disgust me too much. Only you could have gone into business with this kind of filth."

"Don't you think they're worth a couple of your famous bracelets?" Pellegrini asked, hefting the weapon and doing nothing to conceal the fact that just now he was weighing the possibility of playing this hand in a radically different way.

"Just try it," Rossini challenged him. "I'm ready for you. If I kill you in self-defense that won't mean breaking our deal."

"Your fucking pathetic rules," he muttered as he turned away. He cocked the gun and fired a shot into the back of Toni's head, then turned and shot Furio.

"There, all done," huffed handsome Giorgio as he wiped off his fingerprints with a handkerchief.

I grabbed Beniamino's arm and put my lips close to his ear: "Kill him," I whispered.

"No."

"He doesn't deserve this respect."

"That's enough, we gave him our word," Beniamino cut me off. Then he turned to Pellegrini who was watching us, suspiciously: "Now get rid of the bodies."

"You don't seriously think that I'm going to go and dig three graves," he objected with a certain vehemence.

"Figure it out," I retorted. "This garbage is all yours."

We got the lady and left the house. As we walked past Togno's corpse she asked me whether the brothers were dead. She seemed reassured when I told her they were no longer among the living. On the way home, I urged her again not to say anything to anyone, repeating that her silence was fundamental to our safety.

"Whoever you are, I'm grateful to you," she murmured. "All I want now is to forget."

When we got there, Beniamino got out and opened the door for her. Then he gave her a hug and whispered something that brought tears to her eyes.

"What did you say to her?" I asked later, on the way home.

"That not all men are like Pellegrini, Togno, or worse still, the Centra brothers," he replied. "And that her lover's love would help her to heal."

"As always, you know what to do," I complimented him.

"Words that were as necessary as they were empty," he retorted bitterly. "When a woman is subjected to that level of violence it's difficult if not impossible to turn the page. Look at what happened to my Sylvie."

And he burst into tears of despair.

CHAPTER FOURTEEN

I tidied up with the most effective cleanser available to me: fire. Furio and Toni kept plenty of highly flammable products around the house that they had once used for custom production of dentures. Before dousing the corpses, I poured a certain amount into the mouths of those mental defectives to fuel the combustion, after having stripped the house of all its cash and valuables; not that I needed them, but there was no point in sacrificing them to the flames. I also had a good time setting up a scene for the cops, dragging Togno into the cellar workshop and putting a pistol in his hand. They'd find it melted with whatever remained of his bones and they'd play around with the hypotheses and conjectures that detectives and journalists enjoy so much. After dreaming up a "scientifically" reliable reconstruction they'd wonder: "But who murdered the murderer?" and the case would run aground once and for all on that question.

I, on the other hand, would be featured on one of those shows that had speculated for so many months about Professor Guido Di Lello's disappearance. Only I was alive and he was buried in the vegetable garden behind the house I was about to burn. "Whatever became of the respected restaurateur with the shadowy past?"

Let them ask. They'd never find me.

They'd question Martina and Gemma, and the two of them would act crushed and incredulous. Right, my women. I pulled my cell phone out of my jacket pocket and called my wife.

"Let me talk to Gemma," were my only words of farewell.

"Can we come home?" she asked as soon as she got her hands on the cell phone.

"Certainly. The house belongs to you, and so does La Nena."

"I don't understand. What do you mean?"

"I mean that starting tomorrow you're going to be running the restaurant," I replied. "And watch out if you let things start to slide. I'm going to be keeping an eye on you and if you fail to do as I say I'll come back and make you pay."

"We're hardly capable."

"I'm giving you an order, Gemma."

"Sorry, King of Hearts, sorry," she hastened to say. "We won't disappoint you, I swear."

"I'd have taken you with me, but Buratti wouldn't let me."

"That bastard," she snarled angrily.

"With him just pretend that you're happy to have me out of your lives. Act grateful."

"All right. I'll do what you say. But will we ever live together again?"

"Certainly. But only if you save yourselves for me. No men, no women, and Martina must follow her usual programs."

"How could you ever doubt it, Giorgio?"

I hung up. The conversation was becoming as annoying as it was maudlin. Those two idiots would remain faithful to me for all time and someday I'd be able to consider the idea, for fun or out of necessity, of coming back to reclaim what had once been mine. But not before wiping Buratti, Rossini, and Max the Memory off the face of the earth. I could have hired a team of killers and resolved the problem in a reasonably short time frame. But the plan that I'd come up with in case of that partial defeat, and which now obliged me to skulk off the field, meant I'd have to work my way up to the big finale. I intended to kill those operetta gangsters, but only after breaking them and annihilating them and proving to them that declaring their stupid war against me hadn't done a bit of good, that it had, if anything, only claimed innocent victims.

I rummaged through Federico's pockets in search of the keys to his car. I held the flame of a lighter close to an alcohol-soaked rag, which I then tossed onto the corpses on the landing of the stairwell. A blast of heat encouraged me to hurry toward the exit.

I grabbed the bag that had everything I'd need to rise again, and I changed cars. I drove to the Brescia train station where I left the car unlocked, with the keys in the ignition in the hope that someone might steal it. While waiting for the first train to Milan I ate breakfast but soon bitterly regretted it. The pastries and cappuccino were terrible. The baked goods were frozen and drenched in palm oil. The milk was reconstituted from powder shipped from Germany. The only thing fresh and Italian about it was the water that had been added. La Nena had spoiled me, but I'd find a solution to that too. I hadn't suffered all this to give up the little things that make life enjoyable.

At the central station in Milan, I bought the ticket that would take me to my final destination: Basel. There I knew a person who would house me in a secure location until I was absolutely certain that I could move freely. That person wouldn't be a bit happy to see me, much less to have to interact with me for a while. But she was in no position to turn me away.

Then one day I'd move to Lugano and start gradually inching closer to the Signora Oriana Pozzi Vitali. The detailed accounts I'd had from the late, lamented Professor Di Lello would allow me to buzz around her, court her, become irresistibly charming to her. I wouldn't give her a moment's peace and, if that path didn't seem viable, I'd set my sights on her daughter, her friend, her housekeeper, her cook. On anyone, so long as they could get me into her good graces, into her life.

She would be the first to pay. After all, she'd sent those two-bit mercenaries after me. She'd paid them to hunt me down. The bill I was going to give her would be a particularly expensive one.

That thought triggered a painful erection. I needed to work it out, but I was going to have to wait until that night. My soon-to-be hostess in Basel would do everything she could to fend me off because she knew that I'd force her to engage in certain practices that she found unseemly. I, on the other hand, enjoyed them immensely, and the preferences of one's guests, as we know, are sacred.

CHAPTER FIFTEEN

Inspector Campagna only managed to get into the house that the papers and TV stations had dubbed "the house of the three corpses" after the forensics squad had wrapped up its work. The building hadn't suffered structural damage, but the three bodies, still unidentified, had really been burned thoroughly. Campagna, however, was certain that one of the bodies belonged to Federico Togno and the other two to the owners, the Centra brothers, whom the neighbors described as good, hardworking people, if a bit taciturn.

This was strictly an intuition based on the confirmed disappearance of Togno himself, his wife, and the proprietor of the restaurant La Nena, Giorgio Pellegrini. The waitstaff was certain that something serious had happened because he had left no instructions and nothing like that had ever happened before. His cell phone had been found in his house and his wife, who'd been vacationing in Asiago with a girlfriend, said that she was completely in the dark as far as her spouse's movements went.

In Giulio's mind there was no doubt that all these events were linked and that they'd emerged from the illegal investigation conducted by Marco Buratti into the kidnapping of Guido Di Lello.

He searched house and workshop from top to bottom, but the only impression that he gathered was that Toni and Furio must have been a couple of freaks, given the impressive number of pornographic magazines and movies.

When he emerged, he had to struggle to choke back a panic

attack that was about to knock him to the ground, an attack triggered by the wave of rage at having been used by that fool Buratti.

After regaining control of his breathing, he called him.

"How's it going, Alligator?" he started out in a friendly voice.

"Just fine. How are you?"

"Damned worried about the fate of our local *vino novello*," Campagna replied, working himself up. "I don't drink it myself because I'm horrified at the thought that the vinification takes place with the aid of carbonic maceration. Do you know how that works?"

"No, but I'm sure you're about to explain it," Buratti replied, resigned.

"Whole bunches of grapes are placed in a stainless steel tank and exposed to a carbon dioxide-rich atmosphere. Chemistry, modern technology . . . you tell me what that has to do with the age-old art of winemaking. But that aside, the problem is that in Italy the law allows vintners to make it with just 30 percent *novello* grapes and the rest with standard wine. And that undermines the reputation of Italian wine because in Japan, for instance, they drink only Beaujolais Nouveau, which is 100 percent *novello* grapes."

"And all this keeps you up at night," the Alligator said, needling him.

"No, what's really pissing me off is your silence and unless you start talking right now I am personally going to see to it that you wind up in another kind of stainless steel tank, better known as prison."

"You really have a nasty personality, Campagna."

"And you're a dangerous man," the cop shot back angrily. "What's going to tip the scales of justice when I march you into a courtroom to be tried for the crimes you've committed?"

"Why don't we just drink a glass together first and have a healthy exchange of views on the subject?"

The inspector named the same bar in the Vicenza shopping center where Buratti had met Gemma and Martina.

Buratti understood that Campagna knew more than he should, but it still might be nothing more than a coincidence. "I was there recently," he said cautiously.

"I know that," the inspector replied. "The security cameras got footage of you from every conceivable angle, but I'd still like to know what you were talking about with the wife of the now missing Giorgio Pellegrini and her girlfriend."

"Missing? Really?" Buratti asked, surprised.

"Stop being an asshole," the cop said. "Let's meet at Livio's place in half an hour."

"Why do you always pick the worst bars in the Veneto?"

"Evidently you've been gone for a while. Now it's run by a couple of second-generation Chinese who speak our dialect. A splendid example of the integration we're all in favor of," he said before hanging up.

Campagna was the first to arrive and he took up his post. The couple behind the bar knew him and served him an excellent Sauvignon from Trentino that the policeman had demanded they keep in stock, or else he'd shut the place down. A short while later that shameless scoundrel Buratti made his entrance.

"I'm really pissed off," Campagna reiterated when the Alligator took a seat across from him. "And I want to walk out of here with a version of events that's going to keep lots of conscientious cops and carabinieri from having to waste time searching for the truth of a case to which you already know the solution. You get it?"

The ex-blues singer nodded. "I can supply you with the answers you're looking for but I'm not giving you any information about my own investigation."

The cop started to lose it. "Your investigation? Policemen do investigations, at best you gather gossip from the underworld you live in."

Buratti snorted. "Well, just don't start getting too curious about the gossip, okay?"

"Who killed Togno and the two kid brothers?" asked Giulio.

"Have you already identified them?"

"No. It takes time to analyze human remains but I'm an old-school cop and it didn't take me long to get it. So who did it?"

"Giorgio Pellegrini."

"And he's still alive."

"Yes."

"He was the boss, right?"

"Yes."

"Is he dead too?"

"No, he just left."

"Who killed the professor?"

"Toni and Furio. And they enjoyed it."

"And why did they wind up killing each other?"

"The split on a ransom; a rather lively argument ensued over the percentages."

"So there was more than one kidnapping."

"That's right. But the professor's kidnapping was the only one that went wrong."

Campagna finished his drink in silence. Every so often he'd pop a potato chip into his mouth. "What I know is worthless," he said. "I can't go to the chief of the Mobile Squad and tell him that I met an informant in a bar who told me these things. I need a solid lead."

Buratti held up his index finger. "Don't you ever dare call me an informant again, or I'll walk out of here and you'll never see me again."

"You just remember who I am," Giulio threatened. "And what I can do to you."

"Sometimes you're just an overbearing asshole."

"You want me to beat you bloody?"

"You want me to give you a 'solid' lead, so you can go back to police headquarters and make a nice impression on your boss? Or not?"

"I'd appreciate that."

"But then we go our separate ways, once and for all."

"That depends on what crimes you commit. I'd recommend you avoid armed robberies."

The Alligator told him to go to hell with an irritated wave of the hand, and then told him he knew where the professor was buried.

"Where?"

"In the Centra brothers' vegetable garden."

The next morning, with the help of a small excavator, the remains of Guido Di Lello were unearthed. Without waiting for the results of a DNA test, the discovery was announced in a press conference which Inspector Campagna failed to attend because he was too busy hunting for Pellegrini. In the absence of any concrete evidence, he hadn't been able to include Pellegrini's name in the report but he wanted to find out where he'd gone into hiding so he could keep an eye on him and arrest him for the first crime he committed. And in fact, he had no doubts: someone like Pellegrini would never abandon his criminal career.

"It's just a matter of time," he'd repeated to himself over and over throughout the course of the day. Time. The time of a policeman who drags himself from one crime to the next, a cop who gets up every morning and searches for the motivation necessary to go on, fooling himself into believing that the government and the people still have even a shred of respect and consideration for the work that he does.

EPILOGUE

I'd called Giannella Marzolo and told her that the case was solved and that I could finally provide answers to the questions that had been tormenting our shared client for far too long now.

"I read in the news that the professor's corpse had been found. Apparently it was an anonymous phone call," the attorney said.

"The usual tip-off."

"Oriana isn't ready yet," Giannella explained. "I'll let you know as soon as she is. And I believe you're going have to wait for the rest of your fee, as well."

"No problem."

The attorney called back in mid-November. In the meantime, Max was released from the hospital, Christine went back to France to be with Luc, and old Rossini watched over our safety.

The fat man's convalescence, as he followed the doctor's diet to the letter, was an excuse for putting off all decisions about our future. The tempests that had swept over us in those last few years had stripped us of any taste for or sense of daily routines, so now we pretended to be excited to rediscover their joys.

Attorney Marzolo had given us the use of her home for the meeting with Oriana Pozzi Vitali. The Swiss woman had put on a few pounds but there was no doubt that she looked healthier.

"Did Guido suffer?" she asked in a low voice.

"Unfortunately he did," I replied. My clients have a right to the truth, however painful.

I summarized our investigation for her. Every now and then she'd break into my account with a slight wave of the hand to ask for an explanation.

Once I was done she sat without speaking for a long time, evidently trying to let every single word soak in.

"I have one last question," she said. "Did Guido die because I refused to pay?"

"Yes," I replied, well aware that I was being merciless. "The boss wanted to punish you. It was a cruel and pointless act, but he was offended by your behavior."

"And this boss died in the fire that burned down the house?"

"No. He's on the run."

"He's an evil creature, he'll keep hurting people."

"I can't go into the details but I can assure you that, unlike in the past, he's going to have to be on his guard now, because his life is in danger."

"Cold comfort," she objected.

"He traded survival for the truth about your Guido. He was cunning," I explained, more convinced than ever that Beniamino had made a mistake by ignoring my pleas to kill Pellegrini. I was certain that the day would come when we would regret not having broken our own rules.

The woman changed the subject. "I've arranged to pay your fee."

"Thank you."

"And I've decided to throw in the apartment in Padua."

"But why?"

"I want the place to be inhabited by someone I know. The idea of strangers moving through the rooms where I was once happy, however briefly, is just too bitter a pill."

"I'm truly grateful."

Oriana Pozzi Vitali stood up, grabbed her bag, and walked away without so much as a backward glance. Her behavior didn't offend me, quite the opposite. She'd hired me to do a job

and she'd paid me the agreed upon sum. Truth for cash. And
then we'd each go our separate ways.

My way led to Padua, where Max and Beniamino were waiting for me. But I wasn't in a hurry. I wanted to catch my breath.
I felt the urgent need of a woman's love. And the compass of my
outlaw heart directed me to Berlin, where I joined La Triade, an
all-Italian organ trio led by the "mayor" of the blues, Antonio
Santirocco.

It had been a long time since I'd last encountered a group
that was authentically "possessed by the devil's music."

Every concert was an event in which each number was given
a different interpretation. The mayor was on drums, Bob, a
gray-haired bespectacled fifty-year-old with a degree in philos-
ophy was on keyboards, and Babe, just forty and a well-known
photojournalist, was on guitar.

We all became good friends. Every so often I gathered the
courage to go onstage and perform the old songs in my reper-
toire as if I was telling stories. And that's how I met Huri, a
Turkish-German whore in her forties, in Hamburg. She was
pretty, sweet, and irresistibly charming. I noticed how she
stared at me as I recalled a love story from high school, then she
invited me to sit at her table where she was drinking all alone,
and finally we got in her car and fled south, drunk and happy.

Huri actually was fleeing. It wasn't the first time, either. The
problem was that she had done nothing to prepare and her
pimp Günther tracked us down in Stuttgart in a squalid one-
star hotel with an unlikely name: the Edelweiss. It was popular
with prostitutes and the night clerk sold us out for a couple of
fifty-euro notes.

Günther's musclemen had come with very bad intentions,
but my girl managed to calm everyone down by begging their
forgiveness and promising to work twice as hard from now on.
I got away with nothing worse than a cracked rib.

Before leaving, Huri blew me a kiss. "I'm on the street again," she said with a shrug.

I'm on the road again. I left that rat's nest without regrets and by no means proud of myself. My affair with Huri had been a mistake from the start. For both of us. And in any case, it wasn't what I needed. I put the blame on the alcohol and bought a train ticket to Berlin. But I never got there.

Around Leipzig I got a phone call from old Rossini.

"There's a guy who's looking for you. He says he's in trouble."

"Who is he?"

"An old friend."

In our jargon, that meant we'd met him in prison.

"From your tone of voice, it doesn't seem like he's someone you particularly like."

"He's actually a pretty nice guy but he works in a sector we don't particularly like."

"Then tell him to go to hell."

"It's not that simple and after all, this is your decision. This is your problem. He wants to hire you as a peacemaker."

That detail caught my interest. "Fine. As soon as I find an airport, I'll catch the first flight out."

Beniamino hung up. And I started searching for information on the web on my smartphone. Now I was in a hurry to get back. A damned hurry.